The Heart of Jacob

The Heart of Jacob

By

Kyuka Lilymjok

Malthouse Press Limited

Lagos, Benin, Ibadan, Jos,Port-Harcourt, Zaria

© Adamu Kyuka Usman 2017
First Published 2017
ISBN: 978-978-54775-8-0

Published and manufactured in Nigeria by

Malthouse Press Limited
43 Onitana Street, Off Stadium Hotel Road,
Off Western Avenue, Lagos Mainland
E-mail: malthouse_press@yahoo.com
malthouselagos@gmail.com
Website: malthouselagos.com
Tel: +234 802 600 3203

To my wife Maria and my children: Justice, Sunfair and Fairprinces.

Chance rules the world. But let he who takes chance at chance beware.

Chapter One

Three vultures perched on a tree at the edge of a cemetery looked down at the cemetery with the tired and sleepy eyes of overfed carrion-eaters. Below them was a desecrated grave where a dead body they had just devoured once lay undefiled. Not far from the cemetery the vultures were, five pigs that exhumed the corpse the vultures were feasting on were in a harvested cocoyam farm nosing for lumps of cocoyam that might still be found in the farm. It was inexplicable why the pigs which were hungry left the dead body they exhumed partly eaten and went to the cocoyam farm to rummage for lumps of cocoyam.

Nosing through the farm, the pigs found little cocoyam. They were still snorting about when they were arrested by Watto the owner of the farm. He had come to the farm to look for any cocoyam that might somehow still be there only to find the pigs. He was ecstatic. The pigs belonged to Jacob a pig merchant and a moneylender. Watto knew there was little cocoyam in the farm. But, now that he had caught Jacob's pigs in his farm, Jacob would have to pay for what his pigs had eaten. He began herding them towards the village humming a tune under his breath though he was hungry.

There was famine in Tounga. Very few people had what to eat. Towards harvest the previous year the village was attacked by locusts which left in their wake ravaged fields of corn and millet. Only root-crops like yam and cocoyam escaped the attack of the locusts. There were rumours that the locusts ate even the bark of trees. Someone said he saw them in a farm of cocoyam clawing at the ground to get at the cocoyam beneath. Everyone said he had never seen or even heard about this kind of locusts.

If human beings had little to eat, pigs also did not have much to eat. Mercifully there were few pigs. No one except Jacob the pig merchant had more than two pigs.

When there was food, Jacob used to release his pigs to go and fend for themselves in the commons. But with the famine, he has being restricting their movement. There was so much hunger that someone might be tempted to kill his pig for a meal. In fact the hunger he saw around him was such that it could itself eat up a pig. But today unknown to him the pigs had sneaked out of the house to roam about.

Usually in the dry season after crop harvest, goats and sheep moved about the village free of leashes that secured them to pegs in the rainy season because there were no crops that they might ravage. However, while sheep and goats might not have any crop to devour, it was not the same thing with pigs. Cocoyam was always in the farm almost throughout the dry season. There was nothing pigs loved eating like cocoyam. So pigs in the dry season as in the rainy season were supposed to be on leashes or at least wearing rings in their snouts. But Jacob resented all these. His pigs were neither on leashes in the dry season nor were their snouts ringed. He kept complaining that leashes on the necks or legs of pigs or rings in their snouts do not allow them grow fat. When advised to keep his pigs in their piggery and feed them, he would say pigs like people resent confinement. What pigs need to grow fat and breed is freedom to move around not food. You can give all the food to a pig, but if it has to remain chained to the piggery, it would not grow fat nor breed. But everyone knew what he wanted to avoid was the trouble and expense of feeding his pigs. If they move around, he was relieved of the burden. They would feed in the commons and on people's cocoyam. When they had grown fat, he would say, 'my pigs are fat.' He would put ropes on their necks and sell them off, keeping the money only for himself.

Now in the tall elephant grass far away from his house, the grunting of his pigs and the swearing of Watto who arrested them could be heard. The pigs kept turning to go back where they were arrested or anywhere but where it was desired they go. Sometimes they would stop and refuse to move. It was clear to Watto they did not want to go home. They knew they had eaten his cocoyam and so would not want to go to the home of their owner to put him in trouble. His trouble meant their trouble also because he would take it out on them. But he would take them to Jacob's house and make his claim however long it takes him and no matter the toil of doing so. The grass though partly eaten by locusts was so thick that the pigs could not be seen from afar. But wherever they were in the tall grass could be seen by the swaying of the grass as they were driven home. Like sharks in the sea, their backs might not be seen on the surface of the grass, but their presence broke the stillness of the surface of the bush quite visibly.

At home, Jacob the owner of the pigs was sitting on a reclining chair talking in soft, broken tones to Makina who had come to borrow money from him to buy foodstuff.

Jacob like other men in Tounga was a farmer. But in addition to farming, he was a pig merchant and a moneylender. Tounga his village was a very big village. The village cemetery was not more than nine years old. Like most villages in Kobam district, there was no cemetery in Tounga ten years ago. Dead people were buried in their homes. But ten years ago there was an outbreak of diarrhoea and dysentery in most villages of Kobam district that killed many people. The national government of Kobam said the diarrhoea and dysentery were caused by pollution of well water by dead bodies buried at home. So it enacted a law making it an offence to bury corpses at home. All dead bodies must now be buried in a cemetery at the outskirts of the town or village. So Tounga like other villages established a cemetery at the outskirts of the village.

As a pig merchant, Jacob bought pigs from Tounga and other surrounding villages and sold them at Lilong, often at huge profit. Usually he only bought a pig when the seller was in dire need of money. Whenever he wanted to buy a pig, he carried his money bag with him. He did not bargain much as was common with rural trade. He would give a price and tell the seller that if he would sell at that price, here is the money. Saying this, he would show the seller the money in his bag. An impecunious seller desperate for money on seeing the money often had little bargaining power left to ask for more money for his pig. And so Jacob would buy the pig at the price he had fixed. When he bought a pig in such a situation, he was likely to sell it at twice the price he bought it.

As a moneylender, Jacob initially did not lend money with huge interest. Villagers borrowed money only when compelled by necessity and so no one would borrow his money if he charged high interest. But with the coming of the famine, seeing people had no choice but borrow money from him to buy food to feed themselves and their families, he began charging high interest on his loans. Many people in Tounga and the surrounding villages having nothing to eat and having no money to buy food were painfully accepting the huge interests that he imposed on his credits.

Jacob was not a native of Tounga. His father came to Tounga when he was a little boy of nine. Not many people knew where his father came from. His father came to Tounga without his mother. So no one in Tounga knew his mother. Even his father that lived all his middle and old age in Tounga, not many people could claim they knew much about him. He lived a life of hermitage saying very little about himself.

Jacob, dark and hairy like his father, was soft spoken and was not a man of many words. Often he spoke only to purpose and in low, broken tones. The only topic that excited him to much speech was how to make money or become rich. To many people in Tounga, Jacob was as miserly as he was opportunistic. However, despite his miserliness, he never failed to offer a drink to any visitor to his house. His drink was always water mixed with porridge. Some people said his water had medicine in it that would make the visitor come to borrow money from him. But few people refused to accept the water whenever he offered it probably because such an action would be seen as a repudiation of the hospitality of a host. With the famine, fewer people refused his offer of water.

Now speaking to Makina who came to borrow money from him, his voice was soft and broken. Makina had to lean forward and incline his left ear towards him to hear what he was saying.

'You look thirsty; take this water,' Jacob said, giving Makina water mixed with porridge that had gone sour.

Makina eagerly accepted the water and drank it. His throat contracted and elongated as he drank the water in jumbo draughts. Each draught was followed by a loud swallowing sound. After he had drunk the water, he handed over the empty cup back to Jacob. 'Thank you very much,' he said, cleaning his mouth with the back of his hand.

Jacob made a vague sign that told Makina it was his pleasure to extend hospitality to him.

'It is only a fool that goes to a ceremony, eats, drinks and forgets why he is at the ceremony in the first place,' Makina said. 'I have come to borrow money.'

'How much do you want?' asked Jacob, looking calm and calculative.

'Ten thousand bembo.'

'That's a huge amount of money,' Jacob said, running his hand over his bare head the way he was wont to when he had no care in the world.

'Yes,' said Makina in an abject tone. He kept shifting on his seat and throwing frightened glances around like a cornered rat. He desperately needed the money to buy foodstuff for his family. He had food for that day. But if Jacob does not lend him the money he was asking for, he did not know what his family would eat the following day.

'I will look into it,' Jacob said finally.

'My family is dying of hunger,' Makina said in panic.

'Is it that bad?' Jacob asked in a voice that only helped to deepen Makina's anxiety.

'It is that bad.'

'Money is hard to come by these days.'

Makina did not say anything partly because he thought there was nothing to say.

'Go and come back tomorrow,' Jacob said. 'I need to sleep over your request and if I decide to grant it, I need to go and find the money.' His money was always far from him when a loan was being sought. But when he was buying a pig from a desperate seller, his money was always near him.

'I am asking you to lend me the money not dash me,' Makina reminded the moneylender.

'How can you conceivably ask me to dash you that kind of money?' Jacob said somewhat alarmed. 'Even your son cannot dash you money that much. Money by its very nature can only be earned, not dashed. That reminds me, what of your younger brother working at Takku? Are they paying him with whips? He does not appear to have been of much help to you.'

'But you said even my son cannot dash me the kind of money I want to borrow from you,' Makina reminded him.

'Well, well,' Jacob murmured, looking a little flustered. 'Come tomorrow for the money. But don't forget my interest rate is thirty percent of whatever I lend you.'

Makina's heart sank. Though he knew Jacob charged high interest on his credit, hearing this from the moneylender alarmed him. 'Even the banks don't charge this kind of interest,' he protested, lamely.

'Go to the banks then,' Jacob said, angry and alarmed at the same time. He was frightened that people were beginning to compare him with the banks. One thing leads to the other. Before he knows it, someone would say he is not a licensed moneylender and the police would come knocking on his door. He must do something. 'Please, leave my house,' he said, dismissing Makina with his hand.

'I am very sorry,' Makina said, leaving his seat to squat on the floor. People do not beg sitting on chairs like chiefs, but squatting on the floor. As he begged, he was slapping the back of one palm against the other, plaintively.

'Why are you still here begging instead of going to the bank?' asked Jacob, irritably.

'I am very sorry.'

'Do you think it is easy to make money?'

Makina shook his head.

'Our people have a saying that if the scalp has meat, touch your own and feel how much meat is there.'

Makina shifted uneasily.

'Do you know that no bank would give you a loan without a collateral security?'

'I know,' Makina said, sheepishly.

'Where is the security you are giving me? Given your condition, if anything happens after you collect my money, what property of yours do I sell to recover my money?'

Makina did not say anything.

'You can now see the risk I am taking?' asked Jacob with a heavy voice that seemed to crush him as much as Makina. Even without saying it, he knew he was taking a risk. But saying it seemed to make the risk more real. 'Risks must attract benefits.'

'Yes,' murmured Makina, helplessly.

'Do you know how many papers you would have to fill in the bank before you are given a loan?'

Again Makina shook his head.

'Do you know how to even write your name?'

'No,' said Makina, abjectly.

'So you have to hire someone to fill the bank's volumes of papers. You will have to pay whoever you hire since you did not pay his school fees. This may require another loan from the bank. By the time he finishes filling the bank's mountain of papers, you would be long dead. So the money may have to be used for your funeral ceremony instead of feeding you and your family.'

A tear dropped from Makina.

'You now appreciate the big favour I am extending to you,' said Jacob, patronizingly.

'I do.'

'Fine; go and come back tomorrow for the money,' said Jacob, waving Makina away.

On the road Makina met an acquaintance and the two men stopped to comment on the famine ravaging the village.

'This famine came with a wife that is cooking for it,' said Makina.

'While we are yawning…'

'It is belching.'

'It has two heads. It is only the first head we are seeing now,' said the acquaintance.

'Ngu said it has a tail and a horn.'

'And I say it came with a drum. As I am standing here talking to you, I can hear the sound of the drum tormenting my ears.'

'Like the honey bear, now everyone has to lick honey from his own paws. There is no beehive from which anyone can drink honey.'

'Unlike the honey bear, we have no paws from which we can lick honey.'

The two men bade each other farewell and moved on to their different destinations.

Chapter Two

Further down the road, Makina met Nathaniel a bricklayer on his way to Jacob's house. The bricklayer who laid blocks for Jacob almost a year ago, the moneylender was yet to pay him for his labour. He was now going to Jacob's house to beg that he be paid for his toil. He had lost count of the number of times he had gone to Jacob's house asking for his money, but the moneylender had always told him he had no money; that he should bear with him.

The bricklayer was a devout Christian who was regular in church attendance and taking of Holy Communion. Though the Catholic Church has no stringent position against drinking alcohol, the Reverend Father of his church was fervent in his condemnation of drunkenness. Because of this, the bricklayer who once in a while drank gin took care to keep his drinking habit secret. He always bought his gin in Lilong and hid it in his clothes or any bag he happened to be carrying. To ensure no gin seller knew him as a customer, he kept changing gin-sellers. Sometimes, on the promise of a tip, he would stand far away from a gin-seller and send a little child that did not know him to buy the gin. The child would happily run the errand seeing what he stood to gain. Whenever he drank gin, he had an immense sense of release from pretence and fawning before people he despised. It was a blissful feeling he would have loved life to be all of.

Though the bricklayer might drink his gin in secret, often he could not hide his intoxication. Often, when he was drunk, he did strange and embarrassing things. Sometimes he pissed in his trousers. If he did not piss, he was likely to walk around with his zip down. Then he laughed in the most haunting manner everywhere he went. Sometimes he would leap into the air and bellow at the top of his voice.

Most people did not know the bricklayer drank gin because they had never seen him drank even ordinary beer. The smell of the gin in his mouth that would have told them he drank liquor, he always took care to conceal with mouth sweetening deodorants. People who did not know he drank said he was mentally unstable. But he was not known to have attacked anybody even while drunk. When he was not drunk, the only sign of madness he showed was that he spoke alone. But he was not the only person that spoke alone. Many people spoke alone, particularly since the coming of the famine. Sometimes when he was drunk, he would call on Jacob to pay him the money he owed him.

When the bricklayer was not drunk, he might go to Jacob to ask for his money as he was doing now, but seldom said anything to anyone about Jacob owing him. It was wrong by the tenets of Christianity to go about telling other people what one was owed by another person. Besides, it was dangerous to scandalise a rich man like Jacob by talking to people about his indebtedness. Since Jacob was rich, he would always have the means to pay him his money. All he needed was patience.

Unlike most people, Jacob knew the bricklayer drank gin but never talked to anyone about it. However, when he was alone with the bricklayer, he used to joke that the bricklayer should know he could not cure madness with drunkenness.

Makina and the bricklayer exchanged greetings when they drew close.

'Are you coming from Jacob's house?' asked the bricklayer?'

'Are you going to his house?' asked Makina.

'Yes. Is he at home?'

'He is not at home. Are you going to borrow money?' Makina asked with fear and a measure of contempt for the bricklayer. He was afraid Jacob might lend the bricklayer the money he would lend him the following day.

From the way Makina said Jacob was not at home, the bricklayer knew he was lying. 'No, I am going to ask for my money,' he said, haughtily. He hated telling Makina Jacob owed him; but Makina's condescending attitude forced him to.

'You; Jacob owing you money?' Makina said and laughed. From the way he spoke and laughed, it was clear he did not believe Jacob owed the bricklayer any money.

'You can laugh; but I know I am not a money borrower,' said the bricklayer with an air of self-importance. 'I still have my two hands and legs with me. I don't borrow from anyone.'

'Yes, you have your two hands and legs with you, but your head, you know,' Makina said, spinning his index finger near his ear.

'My head is on my neck.'

'Now, yes. And this famine is to be thanked for it. Who has grains to brew beer now?'

So he knows I take liquor, the bricklayer thought fearfully. 'Ah, this world. Nothing is ever hidden from the sons of men. People are always prying into what is not their business. Well, so long as the Reverend Father does not know.' He knew if the Reverend Father knew, he would have asked him. Suspecting Makina was one of Jacob's debtors, he said contemptuously, 'it's a shame to borrow money. I don't owe anyone. Instead, it is the moneylender that owes me,' he repeated, boorishly.

Makina looked at the bricklayer somewhat embarrassed. 'Well, Jacob is not at home,' he said after an interval of silence.

'I don't believe you,' said the bricklayer, moving on to Jacob's house.

Jacob was still at home when the bricklayer arrived. 'Nathaniel, you don't cure madness with drunkenness,' he said to the bricklayer after they had greeted. 'Now, you are drunk.'

'I am hungry rather,' said the bricklayer. 'The locusts flew away with my food. They should have also taken my stomach with them. It was cruel not to do so.'

'I know you have come for your money again,' said Jacob.

'Yes,' said the bricklayer.

'How much is this your money that you will not allow me drink water and put the cup down?' Jacob asked.

'Three thousand bembo,' the bricklayer said.

'Three thousand bembo,' Jacob repeated in a tone that impressed the bricklayer the amount was a fortune. 'Three thousand bembo,' he repeated, biting his lower lips and slumping his head so that his chin rested on his chest. For sometime he said nothing.

The bricklayer watched him anxiously. He needed the money to treat his ulcer which had become very acute. He had the ulcer before the famine. But the famine had made it more severe. The last time he went to the hospital at Lilong, the doctor told him unless the ulcer was treated in the next three weeks, it could kill him. The three weeks the doctor gave him would expire in five days. Now sitting in front of Jacob, he could feel the pain of the ulcer biting through his intestines like the tip of a pin on an open wound. It was not a hot day but he was sweating.

Jacob was about saying something when he heard the grunting of some of his pigs which were now approaching home. His hitherto cloudy face lit up. He stood up and walked towards the piggery at the back of his house to be sure it was the pigs that had returned. He was a light footed man. People said they only saw him after he had walked past them. At the back of the house, he watched his pigs with satisfaction and rare joy. At this time of famine, the pigs looked well fed though they were not. They had wandered about nosing for food but finding little in a famished country.

Now looking at the two pigs that had returned home, he was thinking how much each would fetch him. As he was thinking of their monetary value, he was also wondering where the remaining pigs had wandered to.

It took the barking of his dog at a passing stranger for him to re-enter the house where the bricklayer was waiting with a long and painful face.

'You are still here?' he asked the bricklayer.

'A poor man will always have to wait,' said the bricklayer. 'We poor people have nothing with which to buy favours, but our time and servility.'

'I don't know about that,' Jacob said with the face of a monkey that had come across a banana plantation. 'Come tomorrow for the money. And don't be late. Tomorrow I shall be travelling to Lilong.'

'A poor man is never late for an appointment because he knows no one waits for him,' the bricklayer murmured where he was sitting. With this kind of answer, the moneylender expected him to stand up and leave, but he showed no sign of standing up.

As Jacob stood looking at the bricklayer, he heard the grunting of a pig from the right side of the house. He knew that kind of grunt very well. It was the grunt of a pig in labour. He looked at the bricklayer biting his lips in pains and pity he had never known possessed him. The man had been so patient with him over the money he owed him. 'Wait for me,' he said to the bricklayer. 'You came at a good hour. I will pay you your money now.'

The bricklayer's face lit up despite the pains he was under.

'And you can have two hundred bembo in addition to what I owe you.'

'Two hundred bembo as gift?' the bricklayer asked in disbelief. Jacob giving him two hundred bembo for free? It was incredible.

'Yes, two hundred bembo for free. You came at a good hour; besides, you have waited for so long. You can take the two hundred bembo as interest on what I owed you.'

I will live long, the bricklayer thought. Whoever a miser like Jacob can make a gift of two hundred bembo to would surely live long.

Jacob entered his room to bring the money. Except when he was going to buy a pig, he never carried such amount of money on his body. It might fall from his pocket or someone might pinch it anytime his mind was not on it. Besides, people had a way of knowing he was carrying money with him and they would make one financial request or the other. In his room the money was in an iron box that the key was never out of his possession. Usually before taking money out of the box, he used to argue with himself. But today, he just put his hand into the box and took what he wanted and gave the bricklayer waiting anxiously outside.

After the bricklayer left, a man from another village whose mother had died came to Jacob to beg for money he would use to buy a coffin to bury his mother. The man with a dreary, whining voice looked like hunger had eaten part of his face leaving only part to mourn his mother.

Did the man meet the bricklayer? Did the bricklayer tell him how generous he was and that was why he was begging money from him instead of asking for a loan? Jacob wondered. People are funny. The moment they know you are generous they swoop down on you with their calabashes asking for alms. If you are not careful, from giving blood to others, you would soon stand in need of blood yourself. 'If only you had come yesterday,' he said to the man, offhandedly.

'But she died today,' the man said.

'Well, well, it can't be helped,' said Jacob, looking pestered. 'Yes, I have to watch it,' he said to himself after the man had left. 'Any tree with fruits attracts birds. People think I am a well from which they can always draw water. Perhaps I am. But any well that gives up too much water soon stands in need of water itself. This one has just thrown his pail into the well and has found there is no water. He will tell others bringing their pails. Yes, there is a famine. But my farms were ravaged by the locusts like those of every other person.'

Chapter Three

The locusts that brought famine to Tounga came months ago. It was towards sunset the locusts arrived the village from the east. They arrived in the dark formation of an excited army on a vengeance mission. They moved so closely together that they were united into one band that looked like a desert sandstorm in some places and like dark rain clouds in others. Their buzzing sound had the wailing and whining quality of the wind that comes with rain clouds. Like thick rain clouds they covered the sun so much that it looked like night was falling. But anyone that had seen locusts before knew they were not rain clouds. Anyone that had seen locusts knew the approaching dark spectre was a merciless enemy that was coming to devour what the rain had nurtured for the people to eat.

The locusts settled on every sheaf of guinea corn and millet and like tongues of fire devoured field after field of corn and millet. Those that could not find corn or millet to perch, perched on grass and trees and like those that perched on millet and corn, they ate all the leaves of the trees and blades of grass they settled on. Some tree branches broke under the weight of the locusts.

Jacob was outside his house when the locusts arrived. It was the third time he was seeing locusts and so the frightening sight was familiar to him. Like everyone, he watched the approaching locusts with wonder and trepidation. Like any other farmer in Tounga, his millet and corn were still in the farm yet to be harvested. But unlike most farmers, he had many farms of cocoyam, sweet potato and yam that he could feed his family with. Also he still had the millet, maize and corn of the previous year in two barns and what he had there could last a year. He also had a store full of grains he usually bought during harvest and horde till the time their prices had gone up when he would sell at great profit. Unlike other farmers, he had money he could use to buy food and pigs he could sell to buy food if things got desperate.

By nightfall the locusts had laid the village bare of crops and in some places bare of vegetation. There was lamentation everywhere. But even as the people wept they were picking the locusts into big containers. That was perhaps the only good thing about a locusts' invasion. After eating up crops in people's farms and platforms, locusts became weak from overeating and could not fly. They were then picked into big containers and fried for meat. For sometime they would be the food they had deprived the people of. Jacob reasoned that perhaps if people could be more laborious in picking the locusts, they would pick almost all the locusts that ate their crops and if that happened, little if any food, would be lost.

So as soon as the locusts attacked, he and his family were out picking the grasshoppers into big containers. He meant to spend the whole night picking the locusts into all containers in his house. Those who would not do so did not know the implications. The following day the locusts would depart and they would depart with their crops in their stomachs. But if he was able to pick as many locusts as ate his crops, he would still have his crops with him when the locusts depart. So he stayed out the whole of that night picking the locusts. His hands ached from the labour, but he would not stop. His wife and son were tired and wanted to go home and sleep, but he would hear none of that. If they must sleep, let them find a place where they were picking the locusts and lie down to have a nap. It was his wife that first complained she was tired and sleepy and would like to go home and sleep.

'I have said there is no sleep for any of us this night,' he snapped.

'I am so tired I can hardly lift my hand up again,' whined the wife.

'It is better to be lame with fatigue than with hunger,' Jacob interposed.

'I am so sleepy I can no longer see the locusts,' complained the wife.

'My dear, to be able to sleep tomorrow and the day after, you have to chase sleep away today,' said Jacob with the air of an all-knowing sage. 'With no food tomorrow, there would be no sleep. But you can buy your right to sleep tomorrow by not sleeping today. Before everyone in life two choices are placed: Either to work very hard in one moment when you can do so and achieve prosperity that would save you from working all your life or to omit to do so and have to work all your life for what to eat. You either suffer intensely in one moment or suffer piecemeal all your life. I have chosen to suffer intensely for one moment and that is what I recommend for you. Besides, what are you telling our son; that sleep must have its way whenever it whispers to him?'

'Sleep is not whispering to me. It is screaming at me.'

'It is better that sleep screams at you than hunger screams at you.'

'I just have to have a nap. I will join you very soon.'

'You may lie down on the ground here and have your nap,' he said, indicating a place for her to lie down. 'But as you sleep, never forget that our crops have developed wings. Bear in mind that we have to catch them while we can. By morning they would all fly away and you can't fly with them.'

The wife spread her wrapper on the ground and lay down. Jacob and his son continued picking the locusts. But the more they picked, the more the locusts appeared unpicked. This was discouraging of further effort in other men, but not in Jacob. He was not picking the locusts to finish them but to reclaim what was his.

His wife slept for only a short while and woke up with a start. It seemed she had had a bad dream and it turned out she had one. She had dreamed someone had bound her hands and legs and was carrying her to throw into a well.

'That someone is these locusts,' said Jacob, 'and they are carrying you to throw into the well of hunger. In fact, it is not a well but a bottomless pit without water in it. It was good you woke up to fight the person taking you into the well. Lala, when a calamity like this befalls you, you can't have a peaceful sleep. It will follow you into your sleep. Sleep is not such a new world as we think. We carry our old world into it.'

The wife joined him in picking the locusts. Their son then was also having a nap. Throughout the night Jacob did not lie down to sleep or even sat down to rest. All he was thinking was that his millet and corn had developed wings and would soon fly away. But there is a good side to this calamity he thought as he picked the locusts. The locusts had brought his harvest in one place. He did not have to move from one farm to the other harvesting his crops. But the problem was he had to harvest the big farm in one night.

By daybreak, Jacob and his family had run out of containers to pick the locusts into. It was only then Jacob sat down under the tree in front of his house to rest. As he rested people walking on the road in front of his house paused to speak with him on the calamity.

'I have never seen this kind of locusts,' said the man that first walked past Jacob. 'They almost ate dust.'

'It is so frightening,' said Jacob, yawning from fatigue and sleep.

'The world is changing from what we knew it to be,' said the man 'Every bad thing you know is becoming worse; but every good thing you know is not becoming better, but bad. We are falling into a hole we cannot come out of.'

'What it means is that those of us who want to climb out of that hole must carry their ladders with them as they are dragged into the hole.'

'What do you mean?'

'You remember the story of the cricket and the little bird?'

'I haven't even heard the story.'

'The cricket and the little bird fell into a stream. The little bird looked at the water and said "I am done for." He was swept away into a gorge. The cricket looked at the water and said, "I was not born to die in a stream." He kept jumping and falling into the water but never stopped until he jumped and landed on grass. To climb out of the hole we are falling into, we need the kind of ladder the cricket fell into the stream with.'

'It is terrible! These locusts can eat off a man's head while he is asleep. That was why I did not sleep last night.'

'Well, they themselves will provide us some meals for a while,' said Jacob.

'Pray they don't eat all your intestines. This kind of locusts can suddenly come alive in your stomach and start flying about looking for what to eat. In all my life, I have never seen this kind of locusts.'

'There are always two sides to an adversity: The bright side and the dark side,' said Jacob. 'Those who look at the dark side perish with the adversity because you can't see anything in the dark and so you can't pick anything. So you die. Those who looked at the bright side see something to pick and they would pick it and survive the adversity.'

'Yes, they would survive the adversity to suffer another adversity. The whole life is an adversity.'

'What lies beyond this life might be worse than what we see in this life,' said Jacob. 'Even in this adversity no one wants to die. Intuition is always right. Our intuition tells us that life here is better than life in the grave; that's why we all cling to the misery here. But our intuition could be wrong and life in the grave might be pure bliss. But the vulture you know is better than the peacock you don't know.'

'Such locusts coming from the east where rain comes from is a huge irony,' said the man.

'The source of life is also the source of death if you don't know,' said Jacob, yawning more expansively. The fatigue and lack of sleep of the previous night were taking their toll perceptibly.

'Such vultures and hyenas carrying the faces of locusts I have never seen or dreamed of,' said the man, shrinking his body in fright.

'I too have never seen or heard of this kind of locusts,' said Jacob. 'Grasshoppers forming this type of great army to attack fields upon fields of crops. It is a big wonder.'

'If pigs combined together like these locusts, I believe they will swallow the earth and all that is in it,' said the man in a tone that sounded mocking to Jacob.

'Good bye,' said Jacob. He was smiling at the man while the man was spiting at him.

Chapter Four

Jacob even as a little child of ten had started showing signs of entrepreneurship and great love for money. Whenever he was given any money, he used it to buy groundnut dry-cake and sell instead of spending it like other children. Usually after harvest, millet and corn were kept on platforms outside to dry before being taken into the barn. When the grains were to be taken into the barn, young boys climbed the grains platform to pass the bundles of millet and corn on the platform to a man standing on the barn. The man on the barn threw the bundles of millet and corn handed to him by the children into the barn before going inside the barn to arrange them in a more orderly manner.

After the work, all the children who participated were given two or three bundles of millet. While other children sold theirs and bought snacks to eat, Jacob sold his and bought snacks to sell to other children. He had such love for money that he could sell part of the food he was given at home if there was a buyer. His father not having made much money, used to tell him that if planted yam does not germinate from the head, it will from the tail.

As the richest man in Tounga, the only thing that showed Jacob was rich was that there was always meat in his house. Beside this, he wore cheap clothes like everyone and ate like food with everyone. Whenever he lent money up to twenty thousand bembo, he gave the person a cheque to cash at a bank in Lilong. He could not bear to give the money to the borrower and watch him walk away with it. But if it was a cheque, what he would see the person walking away with was a piece of paper and not the real money. He would not be at the bank to see him walk away with the money. If the money was less than twenty thousand bembo and he was giving it to the borrower, a greater part of the money would be in his palm, while he extended only a bit of it to the borrower. As the borrower took the money, it rubbed against his palm and he got immense satisfaction from this. Somebody had joked that if Jacob were to faint, money should be placed on his chest to resuscitate him instead of the cold water usually thrown on a person that had fainted. If it was feared he had died, money should be shaken by his ears and if he did not stir then he was dead and nothing could bring him back to life.

Initially Jacob deployed a lot of time and energy to his pursuit of money. But gradually he came to an understanding that people who were rich did not work harder than anyone else. Rather they were people who took advantage of any situation that arose from which money could be made. Crops were very cheap at the time of harvest; he bought and horded them until the rainy season when they were expensive and needed more by farmers who must eat before they could work on their farms. He also bought fertilizer cheaply from government in the dry season and sold it to farmers at exorbitant prices during the rainy season.

In his youth Jacob was always at mass every Sunday and was seen by many as a devout Christian. He was about to be made a knight when his church attendances began to drop. The church was beginning to insist on big offerings every Sunday and payment of tithes. As a knight and one with means he was expected to lead by example. This meant making big offerings and paying higher tithes. He could not do any of these. He would pay tithes and make offerings no doubt, but not what the Reverend Father expected. When his church attendances dropped, his belief in the Christian faith also dropped. He found his mind going back to ancestral worship he had earlier abandoned.

Because Jacob bought and stocked grains, when the famine came, he had a lot of grains in stock. Now he could sell his grains for more than three times the price he bought them. There was a lot of resentment among the people against the exorbitant prices he was charging for his grains; but people only grumbled. Having no option, they purchased the grains at the cut-throat prices he was selling them.

Two months into the famine, two men who had just bought guinea corn from Jacob met along the road and as usual began to lament Jacob's outrageous prices.

'A surprise attack overtakes even the strongest man,' said the first man. 'But a battle fixed for a specific date does not consume even the lame.'

'That's true,' said the second man. 'With knowledge of the coming war, even the lame has time to crawl to safety. Look at Jacob; it seems he had fore-knowledge of the coming of this famine. He seems to have prepared for it more than any of us.'

'If it were only fore-knowledge my heart would not be seething the way it is now,' said the first man. 'It might be that Jacob brought the locusts so as to profit from the calamity.'

'I don't think so. Rather I think Jacob is Joseph in Egypt. He saw the famine coming and made provisions for it,' said the second man.

'That maybe so,' said the first man. 'But unlike Joseph, he cannot save his father and brothers from Canaan. He is too mean and miserly for that.'

'You are perfectly right there,' said the second man. 'Jacob is the rich man with Lazarus at his feet. He would rather you die of hunger than allow the crumbs from his table to give you life.'

'Everyone is now borrowing money from him to feed his family. Some are pledging their land for food.'

'But there is no surprise in this if you remember the mean behaviour of his namesake in the Bible,' said the second man with rare gusto. 'Seeing Esau his elder brother was hungry and needed food, he insisted his brother trade his birthright for the food he would give him.'

'There is something in a name. '

'Something sinister and awful. Whoever gave Jacob his name was a seer.'

'A name is a solemn prayer.'

'Call your child a goat and he will behave like one.'

'Jacob has the heart of a vulture...'

'A heart that preys on the misfortunes of others.'

'Well, I will never trade my birthright to this Jacob.'

'Don't be too quick to vomit what hunger might later force you to eat up. You don't know how long this famine will last.'

'I will die first before I sell my birthright.'

'Let's leave death out of it. It is too close for us to be calling its name without looking back.'

'Yes, even his father Isaac, Jacob of the Bible did not spare,' said the second man. 'Seeing his father was old and blind, he wore an animal skin and deceived the old man to bless him thinking he was Esau.'

'Jacob has the heart of a vulture...'

'A heart that preys on the misfortunes of others without pity.'

'No one feasts on the misery of another and prospers.'

'When I look at Jacob, I am not sure of what you are saying.'

'In fact even God did not escape from this treacherous son of opportunity,' said the first man. 'He wrestled with God in the dark until God blessed him. While honest men went about working hard for their livelihood, this opportunist was loitering around looking for opportunities to be blessed so that he would have what he had not worked for. It's the same nasty traits you find in our Jacob.'

'I am surprised people are quick to call their children Jacob instead of Esau. It only goes to show we are all cheats or at least admire cheats.'

'It is bad.'

'There is little gain in the profit that makes another person cry. Someone should tell Jacob this.'

'Since the locust ate all our crops, we ought to have caught enough locusts to fill our barns,' said the first man changing the topic. 'Our barns ought to be bursting with them. Now they are bursting with emptiness. Those who still have the fried locusts don't have to submit themselves to Jacob's extortionate prices.'

'You are right. But you cannot eat locusts everyday. Besides, eating locusts has its own hazards.'

'What hazards are you talking about?'

'You haven't heard how Kadong was stung in the mouth by a scorpion he had thrown into his mouth together with the locusts he was eating?'

The second man laughed in spite of himself. 'How did it happen?' he asked.

The first man also laughed. 'Laughter is good in our situation,' he said. 'The widow said she too was going to laugh when others were laughing, after all she did not kill her husband. We did not bring the locusts; so we should laugh when there is cause for laughter. Like I was saying, Kadong was eating locusts in the night not knowing there was a scorpion in the locusts. He scooped the locusts with the scorpion and threw them into his mouth to chew and swallow. It was in his mouth the scorpion chose to sting him. You know there is no way they could tie the mouth to stop the poison spreading to other parts of his body as they would have if the scorpion had stung him on his hand. As I am speaking to you now, he is still lying at home with a swollen head.'

Again the second man laughed. 'Talking about locusts and scorpions reminds me of the honey bee. You know locusts are just like honey bees. A honey bee would sting you though it knows that means its death. The pleasure of stinging is too irresistible to it. It is the same thing with locusts. Locusts attack crops though they know they would end up as meals for those whose crops they had attacked.'

'I will not say bees sting out of an irresistible pleasure of stinging as you put it,' said the first man, 'but out of anger. Bees sting only those who go to steal their honey or who they find with their honey. You know the labour bees put to gather their honey. After labouring so hard, some idler comes to take the honey away from them. It is so heartless and annoying. So bees sting people out of anger not out of the pleasure they get from stinging. If you have heard about suicide bombers, bees are suicide bombers. They bomb their oppressors and themselves out of existence so that their offspring can have a better life.'

'What you are saying is that bees have more courage than us?' said the second man.

'Without doubt,' said the first man with a rabid sense of sealing a weighty point he felt he had made. 'Bees don't sit tamely by the way we do to be preyed upon by hawks that do not know the meaning of giving anyone his due.'

'The famine has turned Jacob's heart into stone.'

'I disagree with you. 'It is not the harmattan that makes the nose of the dog to run with catarrh. The dog was born with a runny nose.'

'To be fair to Jacob, like the caterpillar, he has never hidden the fact that he is a wizard.'

After talking more about the blight the locusts had brought to the village, the two men dispersed and went about finding what to eat.

Chapter Five

With the coming of the famine, Jacob had tried talking his younger brother who was a carpenter into coffin-making. 'You see the opportunity for making money has cropped up in the business of coffin-making,' he had told his brother. 'As a carpenter you can take advantage of this opportunity.'

'What opportunity are you talking about?' asked the brother a little confounded.

'Haven't you observed the expensive caskets people are buried in nowadays?' asked Jacob. 'Such coffins go for fortunes,' he said, looking at the brother coyly.

'I don't understand,' said the brother.

'With this famine, people are dying now than they are born,' said Jacob. 'Those that have relations with means are buried in coffins. Everything has its season and wise men ride on the season to become rich. This is the season of death. It is up to you who is well-placed to take advantage of the season and become rich.'

'I still do not understand,' said the brother.

'How can't you understand?' asked Jacob, fast losing patience. He was always short of patience with people who could not see how a bembo could be made. 'Who makes the coffins? Is it not carpenters like you? As a carpenter making coffins, this money will go to you. Sometimes because there is no coffin-maker here, some people bury their dead relations without a coffin. Of course it suits them since they don't have to spend any money on a coffin. But if there is a coffin-maker in the village, they would lose that excuse. If they don't have money to buy a coffin, they would come to me to borrow. You see how you and I can easily be in good business in this village?'

'But making coffins is morbid business; I don't like it,' said the brother.

'What do you mean making coffins is morbid business? If you call such a decent, cheerful business morbid, what would you call the business of the undertaker and the gravedigger which young men like you are making their millions from in big cities? There is nothing as cheerful as money. So whatever work brings it is the most cheerful thing I know. Even pastors now pray for armed-robbers if they would bring some of the proceeds of their banditry to the church.'

'That maybe true,' said the brother. 'But I don't think any pastor prays for gravediggers and their cousins the coffin-makers. Let me tell you the story as I heard it in Lilong. A pastor of one of these fanciful prosperity churches asked any member of his congregation whose business was not prospering well to stay behind after service to be prayed for. Among those who stayed behind was a gravedigger. After the pastor had prayed for the gravedigger for the prosperity of his business, he remembered he had not asked the supplicant what his business was. The gravedigger without batting an eyelid told him. The pastor was so shocked he almost fainted.'

'That pastor must be one in ten,' said Jacob. 'If a pastor can pray for the success of an armed-robber that kills, what is there in his spirit to stop him praying for the man who does the decent job of helping get rid of the dead body? If he declines to pray for him, it would not be because he is in a dirty business, but because the pastor feels his business would not bring in as much money into the church as the lucrative business of brigandage. The issue today my brother is what can earn money. If you are to pray for anything at all, pray for money because eventually even the Reverend Father will ask for money before he prays to God to have mercy on your soul when you die.'

'Being a coffin-maker means I will be feeding on dead bodies like a vulture.'

'Perhaps you have not heard the story of the man they called *Carry-Your-Spoon-with-You* that is why you are talking the way you are,' said Jacob, an amused expression taking over his face.

'Who is *Carry-Your-Spoon-With-You*?' asked the brother with the warm ease of a man expecting to hear a funny tale.

Carry-Your-Spoon-With-You is a man who lives on meals and alms given at funeral ceremonies. Every day he switches on his radio to hear who is dead and where the funeral ceremony would be. As soon as he hears where the burial ceremony is taking place, he heads there to have a free meal and possibly receive alms. If he hears nothing on the radio, he rushes to any nearby cemetery to wait for any corpse that might be brought for burial. If a corpse is brought, he follows the crowd back to the bereaved family for a free meal.'

Jacob's brother laughed in a way he had not for a long time. 'What a story,' he said when he found his voice again. 'But, Jacob, where do you always hear this kind of stories?'

'Where I heard the story is not important. What is important is for my brother to know we will all be unable to earn a living if we don't feed on each others' miseries. The doctor to me is a vulture feeding on the diseases of other men. So is the lawyer feeding on the troubles of others. The barman feeds on the spirit of drunkenness in the drunk. The Reverend Father would not eat if there were no sins. Our stomachs move all of us to feed on carrions of different kinds. Without all those things we consider bad providing a livelihood, life would be impossible. We are all vultures my brother if you don't know.'

You might be right, but I will not be a coffin-maker,' said the brother in a voice that sounded resolute.

'Can you still remember the casket Noah the naval officer was buried in?' asked Jacob, ignoring the protest of his brother.

'Yes, I can.'

'How much in your mind do you think it cost?'

'I don't know, but it must have cost a fortune.'

'That fortune would have been yours if you were a coffin-maker. There is nothing morbid about this thing my brother. If anything, it is a healthy business of helping to provide decent accommodation for the dead. It is just like a mortuary in the hospital; only that in your case, you would be providing a permanent mortuary.'

'But Noah died in Dawen and they had to come with the body in a coffin made in Dawen. They couldn't have asked me to make a coffin here and take it to Dawen or brought the body without a coffin so as to use my coffin,' the brother said.

'You are right there,' said Jacob. 'But even here there would be enough demand for coffins to make you rich. You don't have to wait for people to die. You can make them and keep just in case… just the way I see them make doors in Lilong. That way you will not miss out on any corpse that needs a coffin.'

'You are saying I should be making coffins and placing them on display like doors? That's more than reminding people of death. It is like inviting death.'

'What was that?' Jacob asked with a look of mischief. 'Does the mortuary invite patients to enter it? Is the hospital itself saying because it has been built people should fall sick and be admitted into it? What will be, will be my brother and we prepare for it before it happens. That is life.'

'Jacob, when a mad man carries the ark of shame on his head, that he does not feel its weight does not mean his relations do not. Because, they bear his shame, a man's relations must tell him his mouth smells if others would not. Already you have a bad reputation as a moneylender. If I become a coffin-maker, we would be called the two foul brothers.'

'I will rather say we would be called the two rich brothers.'

'Behind you, a lot of people say you are a bad man.'

'Let me tell you something my brother,' said Jacob 'From ancient times, children had thrown stones and wooden missiles at the mango tree to pluck mangoes. Sometimes the leaves of the mango tree and its fruits are plucked by the children's missiles, but the tree survives the missiles to bear fruits again. A war of stones and wooden missiles therefore does not destroy the mango tree. I am a bad man, fine; but that is why I am still alive. Most of my age mates who tried to be good are long dead. The world, if you don't know, is a rotten place and tolerates only rotten people. You are my younger brother; but if you go on trying to be good the way you are, you will likely die before me.'

'You have gotten away with evil deeds and you are beginning to think you are the favoured child of the devil, isn't it?' asked the brother. 'Well, let me tell you something Jacob. It is not the day a man sleeps with the herbalist's wife that he develops elephantiasis of the scrotum. It is much later.'

'From death, you moved to talking about elephantiasis of the scrotum and you said you don't like morbid things,' Jacob said with an amused look on his face.

'To me, death is not a morbid thing,' said the brother. 'It is trying to make money out of it that is morbid to me. It is what you meet on the other side of life after your mercenary life here that is frightening to me. All these people you are lending money to and charging exorbitant interests, if you don't pay them here on earth, you will have to pay them in the hereafter all that you have taken from them.'

'When I come to borrow money from you there to repay them, charge your own interest,' Jacob said, hissing. 'We are talking of how you can be rich here and you are babbling about a fantasy called *the hereafter*. From the way the Father of your church goes after money to live a comfortable life in this world, does he give you an idea there is a place called heaven? If there is such a place he should know more than any of us. He is the man of God as you know. So more than any of us he should know if there is heaven and hell or not. If there is heaven, he would have been less concerned with this world that is brief and more concerned with that world he says last forever. Shake your head and refocus your eyes; remove the film in your eyes my brother and see through the scam contrived to milk you till you die. Wake up and make money here like the Reverend Father.'

'Whatever the money I will not be a coffin-maker,' said the brother firmly. 'Fortune comes from God who created me. My devices cannot hasten its trip to me; neither can my lack of devices delay its arrival in my house.'

'Fortune is a woman if you don't know,' said Jacob in a dismissive tone. 'You have to woo her well before she agrees to marry you.'

Chapter Six

A hunter passing by the cemetery at the outskirts of Tounga first smelled the stench of the exhumed, decomposing body before he saw the three vultures on top of the tree. Even from where he was, he knew whose grave it was. It was Chuwajo's grave. Chuwajo who was suspected to have died of diabetes four days ago was buried in the cemetery at the outskirts of the village. Though the hunter knew whose grave it was, to know what desecrated it, he moved closer the grave despite the rising nausea in his throat. One of the vultures on top of the tree flew away flapping its wings with a lethargy satiation had induced. The other two vultures remained perched on the tree with something near an air of indifference to the intruding human presence.

Bakam – the hunter needed not walk too close to the grave to see it was desecrated by pigs. By his right, he could see the droppings of pigs and their footprints. In his life he had never beheld a horrible spectacle like this. One of the dead man's hands and his face had been exhumed. The vultures had picked almost all the flesh on the exhumed hand and part of the flesh on the face of the decomposing corpse. One of the eyes of the dead man stared sightlessly up at the vultures on top of the tree as if pleading with them to have mercy on a poor dead man. An involuntary scream escaped Bakam's lips on taking in these gory details at a glance. He turned and walked hurriedly away from the desecrated grave and the cemetery. In his mind, he had no doubt it was Jacob's pigs that desecrated the grave. Amidst the nausea he felt was a seething rage. Jacob was getting away with more than was good for him. Unlike many people in Tounga, he did not owe Jacob money and so had no reason to fear the moneylender. On the way he met Nathaniel the bricklayer returning from Jacob's house with his bricklaying money. He was in an ecstatic mood.

'You look terrible,' said the bricklayer. 'What has happened again?'

'I have seen what I never thought I would see before I die.'

'How could you have thought so soon you have seen all you would see before you die?' asked the bricklayer, jocularly.

'This is not a joking matter, Nathaniel.'

'What did you see?'

'It is terrible.'

'From your face I can see it is terrible. What is it?

'It is awful.'

'You are beginning to exasperate me.'

'It is frightful.'

'What is it?'

'I will carry the image of this thing to my grave.' When he mentioned grave, the horror on his face seemed to increase.

'Well,' the bricklayer intoned, appearing to give up his inquiry.

'Something has happened that there is nothing in our custom to speak to it.'

'Bakam, what is the matter with you? You are putting on so much drama over what I don't know.'

'What I saw there is full of drama.'

'Well,' muttered the bricklayer.

Jacob's pigs have exhumed Chuwajo's dead body for vultures to eat.'

An involuntary shiver went through the bricklayer. 'What!' he screamed. 'It cannot be.'

'You are moving in the direction of the cemetery, check for yourself,' Bakam said, grisly.

'You met the pigs at the cemetery?' the bricklayer asked

'No.'

'How then did you know it was Jacob's pigs? Don't bite what you may not be able to chew o.'

'I didn't see them, but who else has as many pigs as Jacob and who allows his pigs to wander about without rings in their snouts?'

'I don't know why people are always quick to blame Jacob for every bad thing that happens in this village. Since when has it become a crime to be rich?'

'Nathaniel what is the matter with you?' Bakam asked with an incredulous expression on his face. 'Is it you talking or someone else? Were you not the one who the other day called Jacob a crook and a cheat? Oh, I now remember you are mad. The demons have come back.'

'What I said the other day went with the other day,' said the bricklayer in a voice short of regard. 'Today is a new day and I am entitled to say new things. Each day comes with its own thoughts.'

'This is incredible, but credible from an unstable mind.'

'It is not good to say bad things about other people, particularly if you have no proof of what you are saying,' said the bricklayer. 'You can be sued for slander. I wouldn't want you to be a guest in the courtroom because the courtroom is not the same thing with a barber's shop or a hunting ground.'

'The footprints of the pigs are still there.'

'The footprints of Jacob's pigs are not different from those of anybody's pigs.'

'I have no proof, but I know it is Jacob's pigs that exhumed Chuwajo's corpse. I can swear on it,' said Bakam. 'There is no one in this village with more than two pigs. The footprints I saw in that cemetery are for more than seven pigs. No two pigs with rings in their snouts could have upturned the grave that way. It is only Jacob who does not ring his pigs.'

'Swearing is submitting yourself to judgment by a force you don't know and can't see. No wise man swears without being forced to do so. For me, I would advise you to leave Jacob alone. He is not the bad man we think he is. If he were not in this village, some people alive today would have long died.'

This cannot be for nothing, Bakam thought. 'What has Jacob given you to engage you as his counsel?' he asked the bricklayer.

'You sell bush meat. So you think only of selling and buying. No one has bought me and I cannot be bought.'

Bakam could not say whether the bricklayer was telling the truth or not. 'You look happy,' he said. 'Have you found money on the road?'

'Am I supposed to be crying?'

'It will become you more than the laugher on your face now. Where are you coming from?' he asked the bricklayer.

'What is it of yours where I am coming from?'

'You are coming from Jacob's house, aren't you?

'Is it now a crime to go to his house?'

'What did he give you?'

'You are beginning to sound like a policeman to me. It is they who ask so many questions.'

'Has he given you food to feed your famished family?'

The bricklayer laughed. It was the kind of laughter associated with mad men.

'That's it, isn't it? Well, let me tell you something my friend; borrowing from Jacob is the worst evil a man can bring upon himself and his children after him. It is your ulcer, isn't it? Do you want to know my mind on the matter? I would rather die from ulcer than borrow money from that usurious, scheming thief.'

'You are panting with hate,' said the bricklayer. 'It is not good for your heart. Take it easy.'

'Nathaniel, I don't owe Jacob a bembo. So I can speak of him as I like,' said Bakam. 'You, Nathaniel are now a slave; so you can't see dirt on your master's head the way free people like me do. I tell you Nathaniel, Jacob is not better than the vultures I saw eating Chuwajo's decomposing body. Right now as I speak with you, I can see his filthy beak tearing open your stomach to eat your intestines while you are still alive.'

'Did you actually see vultures eating Chuwajo's body?' asked the bricklayer, a fearful expression taking over his face.

'What difference will that make to you who have sold your soul to the devil?' asked Bakam.

'Well, you see as I said, we should only bear witness on what we see. Suspicion my Reverend Father tells me is a mortal sin.'

'I don't go to church.'

'That is a sin. But, that is not even the issue. The issue is if you actually saw Jacob's pigs eating Chuwajo's corpse.'

'I will deal with him,' Bakam swore, ignoring the bricklayer's question.

'You have no witness.'

'The vultures are my witnesses.'

'But you said Jacob is a vulture. Vultures if you don't know don't testify against each other.'

'I swear, I will deal with him.'

'Barking dogs don't bite. When a snake spits before it strikes, it loses its war arsenal in the spit.'

Bakam hissed and walked away from the bricklayer. A couple of yards away, he heard the grunting noises of pigs on the left side of the road. He turned and looked in the direction of the noise and saw a man wielding a big stick against a band of pigs not with the friendship of an owner taking his pigs home, but with the hostility of a man who arrested the pigs and was taking them where he would lodge a complaint and make a claim. When he had a better view of the man, it was Watto. 'Nathaniel, come back here!' he shouted after the bricklayer.

The bricklayer hissed but turned and walked back to the hunter.

'What is the matter?' Bakam asked Watto.

'These pigs had finished the cocoyam in my farm,' Watto said, breathlessly.

'Yours is cocoyam they ate. They had eaten almost all of Chuwajo in his grave.'

'Are you serious?' Watto asked, terror replacing the anger on his face.

'I can't joke over a matter like that, can I?'

'No wonder,' Watto said. 'There is this smell about the pigs that I had wondered what it is all about. 'This is terrible!'

Even as Watto spoke about the smell, both Bakam and the bricklayer could perceive it. It was faint, but it turned the stomach.

'See, the red earth of the grave in their hooves,' Bakam said, pointing at the hooves of the pigs. 'See the blood of the dead man on the snout of that pig,' he said, pointing at a pig with a smear of dark blood on its snout. The smear was caking.

'Whose pigs are they?' the bricklayer asked.

Watto thought it was a rhetorical question. Nevertheless he said, 'Who else owns such a herd but Jacob the moneylender?'

'Jacob you have been eating our food in our intestines and we have been grinning at you like servile dogs,' Bakam mourned in a very pitiable voice. 'If a witch is wise, she does not practise her witchcraft in the open. Jacob, you have shown yourself an unwise wizard.'

'Today, he would tell me why I should repay his loan and the huge interest on it while his pigs ravage my farm,' Watto said, foaming on the left side of his mouth.

'So you also owe him?' asked Bakam.

'You don't?' asked Watto.

'No, I don't. Neither had I ever begged him for anything.'

There was a look of incredulity in Watto's face. It was like Bakam was telling him that since the famine he had not eaten anything. For a while he did not say anything. 'Well, you know there is this saying that God creates a contented poor man to humiliate a rich man,' he said at last. 'In you I find the truth of this saying.'

'With me Jacob is as filthy as his pigs,' Bakam said in a haughty voice.

'I think you are the only one in this village that does not owe Jacob,' said Watto. 'I think even the chief owes him; that's why he has not been able to say enough to all the atrocities of the moneylender.'

'You slave, can you hear a man who still knows he is a man though he is a debtor?' Bakam said to the bricklayer, contemptuously.

The bricklayer did not say anything. But inside he was seething with rage.

'Have you lost your tongue? You were very eloquent in defence of a palpable villain a while ago. What is holding your tongue in your mouth now?'

Still the bricklayer did not say anything. By the way he was contorting his face it seemed his ulcer pains were back. But none of the two men seemed to notice the change on his face.

Watto moved on with the pigs. Bakam followed him.

Chapter Seven

Jacob at home was attending to his pig in labour as a midwife would a woman in labour. He expected the pig to deliver as many as five or six piglets. Like a herdsman would give more care and attention to a cow in labour than to his wife in labour, Jacob was giving more care to his pig about to litter piglets than he would to his wife. The pig was lying down on its side, its hind legs curling and stretching as it tried to bring out the piglets. Jacob went and tried to manoeuvre it to a more comfortable position, but the pig kicked out. He released his hold and stood up wondering what to do. After standing for a while, he entered the house to change into a short knickers and a shirt which he felt were better suited for the midwifery task he was about engaging himself. It took him time to find the wears he needed. By the time he did, put them on and came out, the pig had delivered all the piglets. The pig had littered nine piglets. Jacob was so happy that he laughed alone. Not only were the piglets many, they looked big and healthy. He moved close to the piglets to pick them one after the other and clean them up, but the mother grunted angrily at him. He retreated and stood a few metres away from the pig and its piglets. As he stood watching the pig and the piglets full of happiness, his younger brother came.

'Congratulations! I can see your pig has just delivered,' said the brother.

'I feel so good,' Jacob said.

'You seem to be the only one at home,' said the brother.

'You know my wife and the market. She went to Lilong market. I think she finds happiness in the market crowd that is why she is moving from one market to the other. I can't see what she is selling or buying.'

'With this famine, there is little to sell or buy in the market,' said the brother.

'That's true,' said Jacob. 'But you know my wife does not go to the market to sell or buy anything, but to simply wander through it. Like the tortoise, she is a market freak.'

'I learned other women call her signal. As the signal on a railway bends to tell people a train is approaching, so her being seen with a white basin on her head tells other women it is time to start going to a market.'

'You see. And I have never heard this nickname,' Jacob said and chuckled. 'I think the closer you live to a joke, the less likely you are to hear it.'

'Where is your son?'

'He has gone to play football with his friends. Everyone in this house seems to be going after ventures that do not haul in the money,' Jacob said, a doleful look replacing his hitherto radiant countenance.

'An international footballer can buy this village including all the people in it,' said Jacob's brother sweeping his hand in an arch to make his point.

'So I heard,' said Jacob, looking much happier. 'It is so amazing how legs can turn into a goldmine. I may need to tell that boy to take the game more seriously than he is. Perhaps he should leave that school and concentrate on the game.'

'He needs to be able to speak and write English well even as a footballer.'

'What are you saying? What has English got to do with it? Football as far as I am concerned is all about legs and not about heads.'

'That's where you are wrong.'

'How can I be wrong? Does a ball understand English?'

'It is not about the language a ball understands or does not understand. It is about the footballer being able to communicate with his teammates and coaches. Even the playing of a ball needs a good head. Football is as much about heads as it is about legs. Your head must tell your legs the right thing to do.'

'On matters that affect others, you reason so well,' said Jacob, giving his brother a pitiful look. 'How I wish you use your head as well on matters that will advance you.'

'What do you mean?'

'I mean if only you had heeded my advice on making coffins, you would have been much richer than you are today. Look at Chuwajo. He was buried without a coffin. If you had one, you would have sold it to his people.'

'Has he been disturbing you in your sleep that he was not buried in a coffin?'

'No. Do you know I have a personal horror of those boxes? If I must tell you my mind, I won't want to be buried in one. But you see we all need money. Because we all love money no one is ready to give it to you unless he has to. That's why you have to get it from him when he has little or no choice but part with it. The armed robber does his own crudely because he has more brawn than brains. I do my own in a more refined manner because I have more brains than brawn.'

'Where money is concerned you can say that again.'

'In this life there are two types of men: hawks and vultures,' Jacob said with a look of rare insight into life. 'The hawks are those who struggle with their preys until they overpower and kill them for their meal while the vultures wait patiently for their preys to die before descending with their talons on them. I am a vulture. The armed robber is a hawk. I am a vulture and happy to be one. Hawks sometimes get killed while trying to kill a prey; but the vulture as you know has no such fears. Sometimes even the hawk who trusts only to his claws end up as food for the vulture.'

'Vultures sometimes die of hunger after waiting on end to no good,' Jacob's brother interjected.

'Never!' cried Jacob with rare excitement. 'Vultures depend for their survival and prosperity on their good sense of smell. A vulture with a keen sense of smell can smell the aroma of a corpse thirty kilometres from where it is. Now tell me how on any day there would be no carrion within thirty kilometres of the vulture? But even among vultures, there are those whose sense of smell is not so keen. Such vultures may once in a while suffer hunger and who knows, perhaps die as you said. But you know the kind of vulture I am.'

'Vultures are too opportunistic and have no conscience.'

'You sometimes make me wonder if we came to the world through the same womb and if we are living in the same world and see the same things. When a hawk picks on a prey, is it not opportunism? As we are standing here, if food is brought to us and we eat it, is it not opportunism? Tell me any significant achievement that anyone has ever posted in this life that is not from opportunity. As for vultures having no conscience, nothing can be said more to the contrary. When a vulture eats carrion, it is rendering service to it. Where I see lack of conscience is where a hawk descends on a prey and tears its guts open with the prey screaming and squealing until the whole of it goes to appease the guts of the hawk. But the vulture is like a cemetery that gives a corpse a decent burial.'

'Yet people despise the vulture and revere the hawk.'

'All that is part of an unfortunate human psychology against the poor and the weak The hawk is seen as strong and rich, so it is revered while the vulture is seen as weak and poor and so is despised. Ask yourself why I am revered in this village despite my being a vulture.'

'Vultures are nihilists and infidels.'

'There is no creature on earth with the faith of the vulture. If what will be will be is a god, the vulture is the most faithful follower of that god. It waits faithfully on every day to fulfil its promise to its stomach while the hawk roams about trusting no one but its talons and beak.'

'Vultures eat the body and the soul.'

'In that case they take the soul nearer to heaven in the sky. Burying them in the ground only places roadblocks between their souls and heaven. Hindus burn their dead so that the soul can migrate to heaven faster. In Parsee country, I am told vultures are the most revered birds. There they practise tree or sky burial. When you die, your body is placed on a tree and vultures will come and pick the flesh to take the soul to heaven. *Flesh to the sky, bones to the earth* as I understand the Parsees' burial. Everyone in Parsee country revere the vulture because you don't know which vulture will carry the soul of your relation or indeed your own soul to heaven when you die.'

'You cannot be serious,' Jacob's brother said, his voice full of shock.

'Go to Parsee country first before you accuse me of lying,' said Jacob. 'Even here, are vultures not couriers of souls to the sky? You know as well as I do that if no vulture is seen after a fowl has been sacrificed to the gods, then something terrible must have happened in the land of spirits. The vulture as a courier is expected to come and carry the sacrifice to the land of the spirits to whom the sacrifice has been made.'

'Human beings are not fowls.'

'Meat is meat and soul is soul. If the vulture can carry the soul of a fowl to the spirits what is it in the soul of humans that is too heavy for the vulture to carry?'

'Even if it is accepted that the vulture is a courier of souls, this has not helped the vulture. People don't eat vultures because they provoke nausea in them.'

'Who wants to be eaten? I don't envy a thing people desire for meat.'

'Will the day ever come that you will not talk about money?' Jacob's brother said, changing the topic. Jacob seemed to be having it all his way on this topic.

'I think money is the only thing that deserves to be talked about and I don't make pretences about what is in my mind so that people can smile at me.'

'You have a way of steering every discussion to what you want to talk about however unconnected the two topics are.'

'There are no unconnected topics here. If only you had made a coffin for Chuwajo.'

'Who told you he would not make heaven because he was not buried in a coffin?'

'That is all you think and talk about – making heaven,' Jacob said, full of exasperation. 'Why can't you think of making the earth for once? What has the earth done to you that you so much resent it?'

'I think of the earth. But you see life here is so transient that it is foolish to give it the attention you are giving it.'

'Since you believe so much in the hereafter, why don't you hurry there, instead of remaining here and making noises the rest of us do not understand?' Jacob said, hissing so loudly that one might think it was the creaking of a cricket. 'Anyway if you followed what I just said on how people are buried in Parsee country you will see that a coffin is even a hindrance to making heaven. My concern is not so much about Chuwajo making heaven in the sky with God or underground with our ancestors as you making heaven here on earth. If it is about the heaven in the sky, my cousins in the air are better placed to take Chuwajo there faster.'

'We are looking at the same thing and seeing different things,' said Jacob's brother. 'You look at the mouth of a hungry man and see only an opportunity of making money. I look at the mouth of a hungry man and I see only an opportunity to help.'

'You are sentimental, if not naïve, while I am pragmatic.'

'Maybe I am naïve. But I think you are cynical.'

'You can say anything. But the world I see is a world that helps only those who help themselves. It is a world of opportunities and not of sentiments. No one eats sentiments; but we are all fed by the opportunities we have exploited. If you don't know, the world, and I think even heaven supports the rich against the poor,' Jacob said, flames of mischief twinkling in his eyes.

'What do you mean?'

'Remember what Jesus Christ said: "To he who has will more be given. To he who does not have, even that which he thinks he has would be taken and given to he who has." This is a world of reaping from the misfortune of others. It is sad, but God approves of it.'

'You seem to know only the verses of the Bible that support your greed.'

'Say what you like, but there is no escaping the truth of what Christ said.'

'Wealth! When would my brother have enough of it?'

'You know someone said if you are selling pure water here on earth that is what you will sell in heaven. I agree with him entirely because Jesus himself said that as it is on earth, so it is in heaven.'

'You would have been a Reverend Father if you had not taken sides with the devil to quote the scriptures out of context.'

'The devil; where is he?' Jacob asked, rhetorically looking about him.

'Jacob and opportunities,' said Jacob's brother ignoring the rhetorical question. 'The way you think is so frightful.'

'Life itself is an opportunity if you don't know. And since you stand so much in need of the wisdom needed to prosper in this world, let me tell you this story,' Jacob continued with the air of a man who had the lessons of life on his fingertips. 'When a squirrel is feeding on ripe palm fruits, it rests its tail on the unripe ones because they would be its next meal. Working in different directions and putting something aside for tomorrow pays a lot.'

'Maybe you are right,' said the brother. 'But as you have just told me the story of the squirrel and palm fruits which you think would serve me well, perhaps I should also tell you the story of how the snake and the frog can both make things difficult for each other. I believe this story will serve you well if you heed its lesson. When a snake tries to swallow a frog, the frog, would swell its body to make it impossible for the snake to swallow it. This gags the snake immobilizing it. The frog of course is already immobilized by the snake's attempt to swallow it. Thus the snake that tries to swallow a frog and the frog being swallowed end up immobilizing each other. As a predator, I advise you to avoid the type of greed that might turn out to be disastrous to you as to your prey.'

'I hear you,' said Jacob, pulling a face at his brother while standing up from where he had been sitting. 'I have not seen some of my pigs all day,' he said changing the topic. 'Let me go and look for them instead of sitting here trying to persuade you to look at the world with my eyes – a thing you may do only when chickens grow teeth like dogs. I am beginning to get worried. With this hunger sitting like a mountain monster in people's bellies, there is reason to fear. Please, stay here and look after the pigs at home, particularly the ones that had just been delivered.' He began walking away.

'Jacob I have always told you that the way you allow these pigs to wander about without rings in their snouts will bring us regret one day,' said the brother.

'My brother, it is not easy feeding pigs alone and still make any profit from them,' said Jacob, pausing in his walk. 'You see in life you have to be a little selfish and less sentimental. Please take care of the pigs at home for me while I go to look for the others.'

Chapter Eight

Shortly after Jacob left to look for his pigs, Bakam and Watto came in with them. 'Jacob, we all saw you going to the earth priest's shrine and thought you were going to make sacrifice. Little did we know you were going to defecate there,' Bakam said, grimacing. 'Jacob, your pigs have done the unspeakable. They have done the undoneable!'

'What have the pigs done?' asked Jacob's brother in panic.

'Your brother's pigs now feed on human corpses.'

'Human corpses?' Jacob's brother caught his breath.

'Yes, human corpses. They have exhumed Chuwajo's body in the cemetery and eaten it up. Where is Jacob?'

'Oh …'

'I say where is Jacob?'

'He had just gone out to look for the pigs. Oh …'

'If only he had waited a little, we, his herdsmen would have brought them to him in a way he wouldn't want them brought,' said Bakam, sarcastically. 'Well, he will come and meet us in the earth priest's shrine.'

'Pigs eating up a human body? Oh Jacob! Just now I was expressing fears on how he allows his pigs to wander about without rings in their snouts not knowing what I feared had already happened.'

'Premonition. Anyone with a spirit in him has it,' said Bakam.

'This is really terrible.'

'Indeed,' said Bakam. 'As we are talking, vultures are taking Chuwajo's soul to heaven.'

Jacob's brother looked at Bakam with amazement. It was surprising hearing Bakam saying the same thing Jacob said about vultures a while ago. It was as if Bakam was eavesdropping on them. Since when has the idea that vultures take human souls to heaven gone beyond the eccentric and cruel mind of his brother to other men? It was very clear that Bakam was speaking in jest; but didn't his brother also speak in jest? It was so intriguing. Well, Jacob and perhaps Bakam might believe vultures would take Chuwajo's soul to heaven, but what about the pigs that could not fly? Where would they take his soul? Suddenly his stomach started churning. An urge to relieve his bowels seized him. When it subsided, he said, 'if this is true, Jacob your pigs have finally dragged our family name to the middle of their muddy pond.'

'It is worse than that,' said Bakam. 'They have dragged your family name, if you have one, to the middle of a pit latrine full of shit. But that is your headache not that of the pigs because a pig in shit is a happy pig.'

'They have also eaten my cocoyam,' whined Watto who drove the pigs home. 'That which the locusts left, the pigs had eaten.'

'Watto, my brother, the elephant has placed his foot where the footprint of the camel was; so no one will see or talk about the footprint of the camel again,' said Bakam, patting Watto on his shoulder. 'When we are talking of pigs eating human corpses, how do you find voice to talk about cocoyam that was eaten by the same pigs? If the lion and the rabbit die on the same day, only the family of the rabbit mourns their loved one.'

'You can't take cocoyam so lightly; not at this time of famine,' fumed Watto

'Yes, cocoyam is like roasted meat at this time of famine,' said Bakam. 'Still, it pales to insignificance in the face of the grave matter of pigs exhuming a dead body and eating it up. Because of the famine that has made your cocoyam roasted meat, Watto I doubt if you still have cocoyam in your farm. Even our great farmers had since eaten all their cocoyam and you are not among our great farmers.'

'Are you?'

'I never said I am.'

'Well, let's keep that dispute aside,' interjected Jacob's brother. 'Who caught the pigs desecrating the grave?'

For a while Bakam did not know what to say. 'We did not exactly see the pigs desecrating the grave, but the evidence that they did is everywhere in the cemetery,' he said finally, waving his hand about to make the point.

'I haven't seen the evidence he is talking about,' Watto protested. When Bakam first told him the pigs had also desecrated Chuwajo's grave, he believed him. Though he could not say if the dark smears on the snouts of the pigs were patches of human blood or not, the red earth in their hooves he thought must be from a freshly dug grave, and from the putrid smell he could perceive in the pigs, the flesh on their snouts he believed must be decomposing human flesh. But now he must make less of the pigs' eating Chuwajo's body or no one would pay attention to the loss of his cocoyam. Bakam had just said so. Chuwajo was already dead. He who was still living must find a way of getting his due from life. 'I only found the pigs eating my cocoyam and they had devoured the whole farm. What the locusts left, the pigs had eaten. Oh my cocoyam,' he sniffed, 'and it is the only food I had to feed my family.'

'Watto, are you denying Jacob's pigs desecrated Chuwajo's grave?' Bakam asked surprised.

'I am not saying they did not desecrate Chuwajo's grave, but that I did not see them doing so, and you know this is true,' Watto said, heatedly.

'This is life!' Bakam exclaimed, striking his palms against each other. 'You think you know it, suddenly you find out you don't. It is so strange. Sometimes you even wonder if you are not a stranger to yourself.'

Division between the accusers of his brother's pigs had now given Jacob's brother a new buoyancy of spirit. The dark smears on the snouts of the pigs could not possibly be human blood, he thought. Though he could see what looked like human flesh on the snouts of some of the pigs and could smell the putrid odour coming from the pigs, he would side with Watto in denying the offence of the pigs. 'There are people who can still speak the truth even in today's world of lies,' he said. 'Watto, I have always known you to be a man of truth,' he said with a lot of patronage in his voice and manners.

'My cocoyam; what the locusts left, the pigs had eaten,' Watto lamented. 'Koyan how much will your brother pay for my cocoyam that his pigs ate?'

To maintain the division between accusers of his brother's pigs, it would be wise to pander to Watto's demands, Jacob's brother thought. 'You have a right to be paid for your cocoyam,' he said, coaxingly. 'But you know only my brother can answer the question you put to me since he would be the one to pay.'

Greed in Watto was so euphoric that it forgot moderation. 'My whole, big farm of cocoyam was devoured by the pigs,' he wailed.

I have to watch it Jacob's brother warned himself. If I agree too much with what this man is saying because of fear of him supporting Bakam's grave allegations, he would make a demand that might ruin Jacob and it would be difficult for me to later deny I agreed with him. 'Like Bakam, I am beginning to wonder if you still have cocoyam in your farm for Jacob's pigs to eat,' he said in a soft voice that was intended to make Watto not feel so keenly the pricking of what was said.

'Bakam, see what you have caused,' wailed Watto.

'Watto, because of cocoyam you will overlook the sacrilege that has been committed against the dead? Ah this life! It is always there to shock you.'

'My cocoyam,' Watto moaned.

'You owe my brother Watto,' Jacob's brother said.

'What his pigs ate in my farm is more than what I owe him.'

'You are forgetting the interest.'

'Even with the interest. Your brother now owes me.'

Jacob's brother's fears were now confirmed. There could be no partnership between him and Watto against Bakam. 'That cannot be true!' he screamed, his face contorting into a hideous scrap. 'Since when had Jacob become a fallen elephant every greedy hyena in the forest is coming to cart to its cave?'

'Is that what you have to say?'

'Yes. Besides the fact that you can't still be having cocoyam in your farm with this famine biting the way it is, how am I sure Jacob's pigs even went to your farm? You could have arrested them on the road to make your greedy claim.'

Bakam looked at Watto and gave a dry, mirthless laughter. 'Watto you see how things can easily turn against you when you become self-centred and refuse to support the truth?' he said, giving Watto a condescending look.

'My farm is still there; we can go and have a look,' said Watto, almost desperately.

'So is the cemetery,' Bakam pointed out. 'When we are faced with a common evil, we should join hands and fight it instead of fighting for our individual selfishness. United we stand, divided we fall; and happy is the oppressor.'

'We should go to my cocoyam farm now with Koyan so that he can see that his brother's pigs were there and that they ate my cocoyam,' Watto insisted.

'If we go to the farm what do we do with the pigs?' Bakam asked. 'If we leave them behind, those with Chuwajo's flesh and blood on their snouts might clean off this critical evidence or someone would. We need more people to see what we have seen before people start doubting us.'

'What then do we do?' asked Watto.

'I suggest we parade the pigs with the evidences on their snouts through the village for more people to see what we have seen. Later, we will take the matter to the earth priest, the chief and the Reverend Father,' said Bakam.

Jacob's brother did not know what to do. It was important they go to the cemetery and the cocoyam farm now so that he would see with his own eyes what the two men were claiming. But leaving the pigs and piglets alone in the house could expose them to danger. The best thing was to get the pig that had just delivered with its litters into the piggery and lock them up. But the pig was too weak to stand up and walk to the piggery. So were the piglets. He moved towards the litters to pick them into the piggery. The pig started grunting angrily baring its teeth as if it would pounce on him if he goes nearer the piglets. He retreated in fear.

'You have to be careful,' said Bakam. 'If pigs can eat dead bodies, living bodies would be swell meat to them. If I were you I would stay with these piglets here and not bother myself over what is not my headache. Whatever you do, we are going into the village now to show the earth priest, the chief and the Father Chuwajo's flesh and blood on the snouts of the pigs. After that we will bring your pigs back to you.' Saying this, he began herding off the pigs that had the blood and flesh of the dead man on their snouts. Jacob's brother looked on helplessly.

'If we cut open any of these pigs, we will find my cocoyam there still raw and undigested,' Watto said , as he made to follow Bakam.

'So I believe we will find the flesh of Chuwajo,' Bakam said, pausing in his walk. 'That's a fine idea, Watto. Where is a knife?'

'Are you here to torment me?' Jacob's brother cried. 'Look, I am fed up with all your nonsense. None of you saw Jacob's pigs in the cemetery desecrating Chuwajo's grave and you came here to threaten him just because his pigs carry what we are not sure is human flesh or blood on their snouts. Go and drown.'

'Unfortunately all the rivers are dry,' said Bakam

'You can drown in your wells. They still have water.'

'That will bring diarrhoea and dysentery. You seem to have forgotten the last one that afflicted this village not long ago. In fact, you nearly died of it.'

'Away with you, vultures!'

'The Jacobites surely have guts,' said Bakam, looking amazed. 'You are calling us vultures when your pigs had just fed Chuwajo to vultures? This is incredible.'

'When they had just eaten my cocoyam? It is wicked.'

'As for your cocoyam Watto, I never believe you have cocoyam that Jacob's pigs could plunder. Look at yourself, do you look like someone who still has cocoyam. If you get back home, look at your wife and see if she looks like the wife of a man who still has cocoyam. Your case is a poor trick by a debtor to turn his creditor into his debtor. Anything might be tried in this life, but it is not everything that succeeds. On your way vultures! Only make sure nothing happens to our pigs. I have counted them and even know them by name. If any of them suffers a headache, we will wear the same trousers with you.'

None of the two men said anything more as they walked away with the pigs.

Along the road they met two men moving in the direction of their coming. The two men were Gochap and Adubu. Gochap had a big forehead and was seen by many people in Tounga as an intelligent man. Initially, he was a reticent man, but people's respect for his intellect had almost turned him into a garrulous man. Adubu was a short man who always seemed to hold tall people in contempt. Yet, when he was talking with someone taller than him, he often tried to stand on his toes.

'What is the matter?' Gochap asked.

'An abomination that we have never seen its kind since the foundation of this village has been committed,' said Bakam

'What is it?' asked Adubu.

'Sometimes when I opened my mouth to tell people what I saw, the horror of the spectacle I beheld this afternoon ties my tongue around my teeth.'

'What is it?' Gochap fast losing patience with Bakam, asked.

'Jacob's pigs have eaten up Chuwajo's body,' said Bakam, grimacing. 'What they left behind in the grave, the vultures are now having their share in the cemetery.'

'What!' Gochap and Adubu cried in united horror.

At this point, two men and three women joined the four men on the road. The men came first followed closely by the women.

'That is it,' said Bakam.

'I said it when this law that requires us to bury our dead in a cemetery instead of our homes was passed,' said Gochap. 'It is like throwing the dead to vultures and hyenas. Now look at what has happened.' Shee shee shee,' he muttered snapping his fingers in revulsion.

'We were slaughtered by dirty drinking water and instead of our people in government to give us pipe borne water, what did they do?' asked Adubu.

'They gave us a cemetery to bury our dead,' said one of the men that just came.

'Such callousness,' said a woman, shaking her head in resentment.

Now there were about twelve people on the road.

'Can you imagine? We have no electricity and no pipe borne water, but we have a cemetery, have you ever heard such a thing?' asked Adubu

'No, I have only seen it,' somebody said.

'Our case is like that of Kobacha,' said Gochap. 'While big men in government from other towns were putting pressure on government to site one industry or the other in their towns, Baga from Kobacha as minister lobbied government for a prison to be sited in Kobacha. What is a cemetery but a prison for the dead?'

'I don't see why you people are raising so much flak over this matter,' someone said. 'To me, a cemetery makes sense in our case. Dying from drinking dirty water and bumping into each other in the dark, you need a cemetery to bury your numerous dead.'

'Since the government is so good at knowing the causes of calamities, can the government divine what brought the locusts and this famine?' asked Adubu.

'I don't think it is difficult to divine the cause of the locusts. The dead in the cemetery brought the locusts. The dead in the *Garden of Remembrance* are dead mad at us. They are angry with us for taking them out of the village like lepers and dumping them in the bush,' someone said.

'Here the young, the old and the dead have always lived together in one community. This idea of a separate community for the dead is so strange. Very soon we may have a separate community for the old as I have been told is the case in the white man's country. It's all so frightening,' said somebody else

'The locusts might even be the dead themselves. Everyone had said he has never seen this kind of locusts,' said another person.

If the dead sent the locusts, then Jacob's pigs have sent their cruel joke back to them,' said Bakam.

'With people dying everyday from this famine, maybe the government will say we should have another cemetery,' said Adubu.

'Since the law that we must have a cemetery was passed, I have been looking at the sky and I have been seeing the clouds gathering,' someone said. 'Now the rain I was expecting has fallen.'

'Jacob's pigs have also eaten all my cocoyam,' wailed Watto.

'It's all lies,' said Jacob's brother, coming behind Bakam and Watto. After the two men had left with the pigs, he decided to leave the pigs at home and follow them. It was not wise to leave them alone with the pigs. Apart from harm they might cause the pigs, they were likely to exaggerate the harm they claimed the pigs had committed to anyone they meet on the road or if they take the pigs to the chief, the Reverend Father or the earth priest. 'Those who envy my brother's wealth are up in arms against him. But we will show them that it is futile for the tongue to attempt to cut the teeth.'

'Not so easily done,' said Bakam. 'The blood and flesh of the dead man on the snouts of your pigs and the smell of a dead body your pigs carry with them like the breath of a skunk have roped you in. The red earth in the hooves of your pigs and their footprints at the cemetery have not helped you either.'

Now almost everyone could smell a faint stench coming from the pigs and could see what looked like human skin on the snouts of some of the pigs. The dark smears on the snouts of the pigs many people did not think were human blood. When the people were expressing their disenchantment with the government over its failure to supply them basic amenities, most people did not perceive the smell. But now that their attention had returned to the pigs, the stench the pigs carried with them acquired a new virulence. The stomachs of some of the people began to churn.

'Now, we will go to the Father to report the mischief in my farm after which we will go to the cemetery to see the sacrilege the pigs had committed,' said Watto who was a devout Christian. Every year, the church expected tithes from the produce of his land during harvest. So the Father was more likely to give him a sympathetic hearing.

'Was it the god of the Father that was offended?' someone asked. He was one of the many men that still worshipped Bosuu the god of the earth.

'To my mind, the god of the Father was rather a beneficiary,' said Bakam. 'The pigs have taken what belonged to Bosuu the god of the earth and given to vultures who had taken it to the god of the sky – the Father's god. No, we will go to the earth priest whose god has been offended.'

'You are just coming into this matter,' said Watto, addressing the man who challenged him when he said the matter should be taken to the Father. 'I have followed this matter right from my farm to this place. Do not begin to think you can impose on us where we will report what we first saw. It is to the Father we are taking the pigs.'

'We are not going to any Father or earth priest,' Jacob's brother said, defiantly. 'What is the use? Let's go to the court at Lilong. The court exists to handle disputes like this.'

'You want us to go to court so that we will spend the rest of our lives chasing the wind?' said Watto. 'Koyan, no one is going to court. The court is not one of us. We should be able to solve our problems ourselves.'

'We are not going to any court,' said Adubu. 'My son living in the city told me that when a thief is caught, he runs into a police station for cover. Though we don't have a police station here, we all know how crooked policemen are. If a thief runs into their station and gives them part of what he has stolen, they would put what they have been given in their pockets and take the thief to the court leaving the person whose property was stolen yawning for the rest of his life outside their station and the court. Koyan wants us to go to court so that he and his brother would end up laughing at us. No; we won't go to any police station called the court. We will solve our problems ourselves. What has happened is outrageous. We will use our anger to purge it, not the order of the court.'

'If you won't go to any of the places we are taking the pigs, don't go,' said Bakam. 'Also when your brother is summoned by the earth priest, the chief or the Father, let him not go.'

It would be wise to go with them Jacob's brother thought. 'It is always better to be where you are accused than absent only to go for defence.'

Chapter Nine

The bricklayer on his way home was thinking of what he would do to help Jacob who had unexpectedly paid him his money and given him two hundred bembo as interest. Who knows other favours Jacob may yet extend to him in future? Since Jacob gave him the money, the pain from his ulcer seemed to have abated a great deal. It was like the ulcer seeing he now had means of surgically removing it, it had retreated so that it would not be excised from his body. It reminded him of his radio which last year was not working and he took it for repairs only for it to start working when he got to the radio repairer's shop. People and machines can feign sickness. As soon as you call off their bluff, they become healthy again. But his body was not feigning ulcer. He had one and must deal with it now that he had the means.

But first he must find a way of helping Jacob out of the mess his pigs had dragged him. He was further moved to save Jacob from the humiliation that would follow the discovery of what his pigs had done by Bakam's arrogance and self-righteousness. Bakam had spoken and behaved as if he had never done wrong. Did Jacob send the pigs to desecrate the grave? What would Bakam have done if Jacob had desecrated the grave himself? It would be good to embarrass Bakam by going to the cemetery and obliterating all traces of the pigs' visit and putting him on the defensive. He had a clear mind of what to do. He would help Jacob out of the mess and implicate Bakam so that next time, if he survives this treachery, he would learn not to open his mouth so wide on what does not concern him. He was only a bricklayer but knew a few things about hunters. He would use what he knew about hunters to deal with Bakam. Who said he could not be a hunter himself after he had destroyed Bakam. At this time of famine there was no lucrative business like hunting. Maybe that was why Bakam was becoming swollen headed. He would cut him to size. If Bakam was out of the way, business would really be good for him as a hunter. Bakam had always exhibited towards him the same kind of boorish attitude he exhibited today. It was now time for a showdown with him.

'People say I am mad, I will do a mad thing today,' he muttered. 'I will do something that will shock the sane. People in the way they look at me show contempt to me because they think I am mad. Today, I will show contempt to Bakam so that he will learn to respect mad men.'

Having resolved to deal with Bakam, he began walking hastily home to get what he needed to achieve what he intended to do. When he got home, he took some ash from the hearth of his house, a knife and a piece of white cloth. He hurried to the cemetery which was a bit far from his house. As he drew near the cemetery, he kept looking back now and then to ensure no one was following or watching him going to the cemetery. When he got to the cemetery, he was horrified by what he saw. The vultures were still there. From the homely air and freedom he observed about them, they had not appointed the day they would leave the cemetery. After he had taken in the grisly details of the horrendous scene, he went to work. He quickly removed the pigs' droppings he could see by the desecrated grave. Using his knife, he cut a shrub and used it to obliterate the footprints of the pigs he could see. After this, he went into the task that he dreaded most. Using the white cloth with him, he tied his mouth and nose and moved towards the half exposed corpse. He pulled out the hand that had not been eaten by the vultures and cut the central muscle which was believed to make a hunter's hand unerring in shooting games. He then poured some ash where he had cut the muscle and hurried away, taking care he did not leave behind anything that would show he had visited the boneyard.

On his way home, a little wind swirled past him towards a bammo tree. Close to the tree, the wind stopped and hopped around one spot like a one-legged cripple. It appeared undecided whether to go to the bammo tree or elsewhere. Finally, it seemed to have changed its mind of going to the bammo tree and headed for the cemetery. Was it going to find out what he had done at the burial ground and tell the earth priest?

When he got home, he was sweating and panting. But he was happy with what he had done. He had now with him the muscle that would make him a great hunter and more importantly, Bakam was now in trouble. Though the pains of his ulcer were beginning to come back, he laughed. He was sure that very soon the whole village would come to the cemetery to see the havoc Jacob's pigs and the vultures had wrecked. That would be when Bakam's troubles would start.

But it soon struck him that Bakam was likely to be the one to lead the village to the cemetery. If that was the case, doubt would be raised concerning his culpability. For he could not desecrate the grave and leave behind damning evidence only to go and bring the village to come and see what he had done. Even an idiot would not do that and Bakam was not an idiot. He started sweating profusely and his heart was thumping wildly. The pain from his ulcer seemed to be increasing. In a moment of blind hate and vindictiveness, he had without thought rushed to the cemetery to do things that would implicate Bakam. Clearly he would not succeed if Bakam leads the people to the cemetery. If that happens, suspicion would be kindled in the minds of many people that someone had attempted clearing the pigs from blame by going to the cemetery to do what he did. Given his spirited defence of the pigs on the road and the fact that he was moving in the direction of the cemetery after he parted with Bakam and the pigs, he would be a prime suspect. Someone standing near him could hear the beating of his heart.

It was too late to go back to the cemetery to undo what he did. For all he knew, the whole village might be in the cemetery now. Well, the only good thing was that given the hurried way he tried to obliterate the pigs' visit to the cemetery, he must have still left some evidence of their visit. If the ash which would be taken as gunpowder was not seen, the pigs might still carry the blame for the desecration. But how would the ash not be seen? He had sprinkled some earth over the ash, but he knew he did not completely conceal it.

If the village was not there already, his only hope was to do something that would make Bakam refuse to go to the cemetery. But what could he do? If he did anything that would discourage Bakam from going to the cemetery with other people and it was known he did it, he would have nailed his own coffin with his own hands. But he must do something. There was only one thing he could do with less risk of its being traced to him. The slough of a snake was a bad omen among hunters. No hunter saw it on his way and continued his journey. He had a snake slough in his house. He would place it where Bakam would see it. Immediately he took the snake slough and set out again. This time he won't follow the road again. That would be stretching his luck too far. He would follow the bush, but move close to the road. If there were people in the cemetery or the road, he would see them. The snake slough was in his hand delicately wrapped in the white cloth he earlier went to the cemetery with.

In the bush, the cloud of desolation cast on the country by the plague like *the ghost of Makpa* whispered into the ears of anyone that strayed into the bush. The locusts left the bush in tatters and nothing had happened to stitch the tears left behind by them. In fact the famine they left behind seemed to further shred the country to tears. Shrubs with leaves looked like mummies in a shroud. Those without leaves looked like ghosts. The shadow left behind in the bush by the plague was still very long. Anyone passing through the bush could see that a plague had visited the land and left behind a ghost that was walking the bush without pity.

The bricklayer walked past the cemetery and was happy to see nobody. But could they have come and gone? Impossible! It was not long he left the graveyard. People are like vultures. They like hanging around rotten places and rotten happenings. From what he knew of people, some of them would not mind remaining in the cemetery for the rest of the day talking over and over again the desecration of the grave and looking for more lurid details of the sacrilege. The people's penchant for gruesome happenings which would make it impossible for them to have come to the cemetery and gone was cheering, but was also frightful to him. It meant when eventually they come, they would spare no time and no mischief in getting all the unseemly details of the sacrilege. This meant he must stop Bakam from going to the cemetery so that whatever was found in the graveyard would be hung around his neck. He had to find out where Bakam was now so that he could place the slough where he would not miss it. Wherever the hunter was, was bound to be noisy. By now, he would be carrying the whole village with him. He began moving faster but listening for the noise of an angry crowd. He first moved in the direction of Jacob's house. There was only one person he saw on the way before he got to Jacob's house. It was a woman who was returning from the forest with firewood. He ducked behind a tree so that the woman did not see him. That people were not about meant the whole village was now where Bakam was. When the woman walked past him, he continued his journey. At Jacob's house, he heard no noise. He sneaked to Bakam's house. There he also heard nothing. It meant Bakam and the crowd had taken the sacrilege to authority and there were three authorities in the village: the chief, the Reverend Father and the earth priest. They were the tripod on which the village sat. But two legs of this tripod were weak.

Everyone knew the chief was an opportunistic fellow that would look at any matter brought before him in terms of how he would benefit from it, not necessarily how the complainant would. Tounga had no chief until the white man came to Kobam and appointed chiefs to collect taxes for him. Now there were no taxes to collect and the chief was hungry. A rich man in his domain could buy the chief with small potatoes. In Tounga, Jacob was more of a chief than the chief. There was little the Father could do than pray for the forgiveness and remission of sins on earth and in heaven. That left only the earth priest who was firm and unremitting in his abhorrence of sacrilege and insistence on justice.

The earth priest had more followers than the church. When Christianity first came, many people flocked to it. But later most of the people that converted to the new faith returned to the old faith and that was how the earth priest came to have more followers than the church. On a serious matter like this, even the few people that were Christians would rather it was taken to the earth priest than to the Father. Of course none of them would openly say so for fear of being called an unbeliever. But their lack of protest when a matter like this was referred to the earth priest instead of the Reverend Father said something. So the bricklayer thought the people were more likely to be in the earth priest's shrine than in either the Father's house or the chief's court.

Chapter Ten

The crowd first went to the Reverend Father's house. Though a crowd of disparate people, it was united by a common feeling of resentment over what had happened.

'Pigs and vultures eating human flesh demystify life,' said Gochap. 'If anyone had told me I will live to the time a thing like this would happen, I would have said he is lying.'

'What will a man tell his ancestors if he arrives before them with half of him eaten by pigs and vultures?' someone said.

'Even the god of the Christian faith with all his liberalism will not accept a man that has been half-eaten by pigs and vultures,' said another person.

Many people began to speak all at once.

'Whenever I look at the snout of a pig, what I see is sacrilege.'

'Even among animals, a pig is an outcast.'

'Jacob, your pigs have thrown us into a well without anything to hold to.'

'You give loans to us that we cannot pay until we die. When we die, you send your pigs after us to eat what you could not.'

'This is like urinating on the dead.'

'Jacob your gain has always been our loss.'

'While living, we pay taxes to you. Dead, we pay taxes to your pigs.'

'You don't even allow us to give to Caesar what is Caesar's; you take everything.'

'I believe it was after the pigs finished eating the dead man's body that they called the vultures. You know they are cousins.'

'Life is a journey downhill. You are supposed to be totally out of sight when you enter your grave. But Jacob's pigs would still have their eyes on you and they will come for you where you are.'

'Life is indeed a climb down a hole, not a ride up a hill.'

'This happening has knocked the bottom out of our patience.'

'Things are getting out of hand.'

'And may soon get out of reach.'

'Our hands are so full of material desires that we have no hands to hold those things you are saying are getting out of hand.'

Bakam and the crowd did not meet the Father in the parish house. Impatient as they were, they began moving to the chief's house. It was on the way to the chief's house that they met the Father in his white cassock.

'Father, the devil has scored against us again. Jacob's pigs and vultures have opened up Chuwajo's grave and ate up his body,' someone cried on sighting the Father.

'The devil is always scoring against us because our conscience which supposed to be the goalkeeper at the goalpost is hardly there,' said Gochap.

'What can a goalkeeper do against a sharp shooting striker like the devil without good defenders? Our values which use to protect the conscience are no more,' somebody said.

'Even the midfield has collapsed. Chiefs, religious people who used to preach and stand by our values have all abandoned their roles to chase money and status,' said Adubu.

Again everyone began to speak without observing the order of conversation.

'I believe the demons that Christ sent to go and enter the pigs are still in them. That is why I don't eat pork. Whoever eats pork is eating demons.'

'It is not what a man eats that defiles him but what comes out of his mouth?'

'How do you expect what comes out of his mouth to be clean if what goes into it is dirty? We need to use our heads when reading the scriptures.'

'How do you expect fragrance from the mouth of a man eating shit?'

'In a refuse dump you can only find rats.'

'From the latrine you can only expect flies.'

'Well, Father that is how it is, what do we do to cleanse the land?'

The Father made the sign of the cross and raised his rosary to his heart. For a while he mumbled something before he began to speak audibly. 'God is concerned only with the soul of man, not his body,' he said. 'The soul of Chuwajo if he was a good Christian is already with the Lord. It matters not what happens to his body. If he was a bad Christian, his soul will not stand better before Christ if his body was eaten by rams, if they can meat. Speak not of cleansing the land, but yourselves of your iniquities,' he said, punching the air with his fist. 'As for the land, it will always be filthy because it was made of filth.'

'The earth was made of filth?' someone asked in a shocked tone.

'Yes,' answered the Father.

'No wonder Noah's flood could not wash the earth clean,' said another person. 'But if Noah's flood could not wash the earth, I wonder how the blood of Jesus Christ can wash away the sins of all men on earth,' said Gochap.

'Jesus is a miracle.'

'I agree. But even he needed water to perform his miracles. So water itself is a miracle,' said Gochap.

'What do we do to Jacob, Father?' someone asked.

'Vengeance is the Lord's.'

'And the anguish is ours. It is so funny,' said Adubu, cynically.

'I thought the person who enjoys the vengeance should carry the anguish,' somebody said.

'I thought that is giving to Caesar what is Caesar's,' said another person.

'You are speaking blasphemy,' said the Father, 'and that is a mortal sin.'

'Well, we will go to the chief,' said Bakam. 'Not that we expect much from him.'

'That is not true,' someone said. 'We can expect something from the chief if there is something in it for him. You know how opportunistic he is.'

'If anyone is missing the white man, it's the chief. When the white man was here, there were so many opportunities for him to live off us. He was so powerful. Now, the chief looks like a child whose mother went to the market but refused to return,' said Bakam.

'That is where the Father is better off than the chief,' said Gochap. 'The white man left the Father with a Bible from which he can still feed. He left the chief with nothing.'

'That is not true. He left the chief with a long cap and a stick,' someone said.

'Only that there is no one he would raise his stick against,' said another person.

'The main problem of the chief now is that there is no role for him. He moves about in his long cap and big gown like a clown while his office says he is a man of majesty,' said Adubu.

'You may go to the chief. But don't go to the earth priest,' said the Reverend Father. 'The Christians among you know the position of the Bible concerning fetish practices and superstition. Any Christian that goes to the earth priest should consider himself excommunicated from the church.'

'But why is Christianity so much against superstition and fetish practices? Are they eating from the same calabash with it?' someone asked.

'Yes, they eat from the same calabash with it by setting up other gods,' said the Father. 'They don't allow you use your heads, but delight only in stoking the fires of your fears. Christianity is the only religion that liberates the heart from fear and allows people use their heads.'

'Yes,' said a Christian among the crowd. 'Christianity is a wonderful religion. Unlike ancestral worship, Christianity allows people to scrutinize it because it has sufficient reason and logic in it.'

'Adam was the first man isn't it?' asked a man who was not a Christian.

'Yes,' a Christian answered, enthusiastically.

'Whose daughter did Cain his son marry?'

'Beware man, the devil is leading you to destruction,' a voice cried out.

'It is a dangerous thing for any religion to allow for any scrutiny of it even if it has reason and logic working for it,' said the non-Christian; 'because all religions in the end have to rely on myths and dogma for their survival and ultimate authority.'

The Reverend Father displeased with what the crowd was saying dismissed it and walked away.

The crowd moved to the chief's house. They met the chief at home.

'Well, chief, this is what Jacob's pigs have done,' said Bakam who spoke for the crowd. 'Our land has been desecrated.'

'Desecration of land is something for the earth priest,' said the chief. 'My concern is the people. I am chief over people, not over land. 'Where is Jacob himself?' asked the chief without the feeling of outrage some of the people in the crowd might have expected.

'We went to his house, but met only his brother who is here with us,' said Watto. 'The pigs had also eaten my cocoyam.'

'I refuse to believe you still have cocoyam in your farm at this time of famine when even farmers more prosperous than you are looking for what to eat,' said the chief, giving Watto a demeaning look.

'I swear I still have cocoyam in my farm,' said Watto, desperately.

'If you insist, that is a matter for the court,' said the chief. 'You can take your complaint to the court at Lilong.'

'The land has been desecrated,' somebody lamented. 'How do we appease the land?'

'No, it is not the land that is desecrated. It is Jacob that is desecrated,' another person said.

'Is it only today Jacob is desecrated? As far as I am concerned, the man was born desecrated,' someone said.

Many people began to speak at the same time again.

'This is the kind of sacrilege that makes the sky to withhold rain.'

'It is the sort of thing that makes the land go barren.'

'Chief, what shall we do about the land that has been desecrated?'

'Land; haven't I told you I am not chief over land but over people?' said the chief, looking a little crossed. 'If your concern is about the land, you know who knows the secrets of the land and how to appease it. Take your concern about the land to him and stop pestering me. But I am interested in how the desecration of the cemetery will affect my people and I shall make my pronouncement on that.' As he spoke, some people said they saw flames of mischief and greed flickering in his eyes.

'The chief is right,' whispered someone to his neighbour. 'If anybody has not paid his tax, he should be brought to the chief. Jacob has not being paying his taxes.'

'There are no more taxes and you know it,' said the neighbour.

'You should know the type of taxes I am talking about.'

'Where did you say Jacob is?' asked the chief again.

'We don't know,' said Bakam. 'All we know is that he was not at home when we went to his house.'

'I will pronounce my judgment even in his absence,' said the chief.

A hush fell on the crowd. No one expected judgment would come so fast.

'But Jacob is not here and you have not seen how Chuwajo's grave was desecrated by the pigs,' protested Jacob's brother as the chief was about to speak.

'What was that?' asked the chief in disbelief.

'I said Jacob ought to be here to defend himself of the charge against his pigs and you as a judge ought to see the desecrated grave before you give judgment,' said Jacob's brother, in a leveled voice.

The chief looked embarrassed. For a while, he did not say anything.

'Koyan is right,' said someone amidst the silence that engulfed the crowd.

'He is not right,' said another person. 'Jacob's pigs are here. They can defend themselves. They desecrated the grave.'

'That is true,' said another person. 'Even if Jacob were here, there is little he can say. He did not desecrate the grave.'

'Who owns the pigs?' someone asked.

'Stop the foolery,' said the chief, losing most of his initial royal air. 'Koyan you are here. What have you to say in defence of the pigs?'

'Nothing,' said Koyan. 'Until I see the grave I cannot say anything. Like everyone else here, I only heard that Jacob's pigs desecrated Chuwajo's grave. I have not seen the desecration myself.'

'Koyan is right,' said the chief. 'We have to delay judgment till we see the grave.'

'The chief is right,' said someone. 'Let's go to the earth priest's shrine now and tell him what has happened. Tomorrow we can all go to the cemetery to see what the pigs did.'

'But I fear for Chuwajo,' somebody said. 'Before we go to the cemetery tomorrow, the vultures would have eaten all of him. In fact even Jacob's pigs might return to the cemetery in the night and finish what they had started.'

'You are saying the pigs might return in the night, they might be there now. It is not all Jacob's pigs that are here,' said another person.

'What of the hyenas? We seem to have forgotten what they can do to Chuwajo,' said Gochap.

There was an uproar of apprehension in the crowd.

'No one will go to the cemetery now,' said the chief, licking his lips like a man that had just finished eating food. Later some people said they saw mischief perched on the left side of his mouth like a butterfly while he spoke. 'The sun has already set. Very soon it will slip into the womb of the sky,' he continued. 'If we go to the cemetery now, night will find us there. We all know that nighttime is the daytime of the dead. Now that a grave has been desecrated, the dead will certainly be up in arms against anyone that moves near the cemetery in the night.'

The fear that engulfed the crowd was palpable.

'Let's leave going to the cemetery till tomorrow morning,' someone said. 'But we can go to the earth priest's shrine now. Whatever the pigs, the hyenas and the vulture do in the course of the night, tomorrow when we get to the cemetery we shall see.'

Everyone agreed with the man who had just spoken. The people began trooping out of the chief's house.

Chapter Eleven

Jacob went to look for his pigs in a marshy land he knew they frequented. It was a land with many farms of cocoyam and muddy ponds the pigs usually rolled in.

Like he had suspected, on his way to the marshy land, he saw the footprints of the pigs in two sandy places, and in another place, their faeces. All these meant the pigs had gone to the marshy land as he had thought. Now sure of where to find the pigs, his mind switched to the two hundred bembo he gave the bricklayer. How could he have been so profligate to give such a huge sum of money to someone as a gift? Surely, the bricklayer must have practised diabolism on him. Otherwise, how could he have been so foolish to part with such money? The moment he returned home, he would send for the bricklayer and ask him to return the money because something had just cropped up that needed money. He only hoped the bricklayer would not say he had spent the money or even deny receiving it from him in the first place. 'He dares not,' he swore, beginning to sweat. Maybe he should suspend the search for the pigs and go after the bricklayer before he uses the money to treat his ulcer. For all he knew, the bricklayer was already on his way with the money to Lilong hospital to treat his ulcer. He felt weak and faint. He had never acted so stupidly in his life. Money is the instrument you use to control people. When you part with it without strings the way he had done today, you lose control of the person you have parted with the money to. Such a person may even go and set up his own court with his own courtiers since he now has his own money. The bricklayer may never come to him again for anything or even greet him when they meet on the road. There was nothing he cherished like people coming to his house, bowing before him seeking one favour or the other. He would sit on his chair acknowledging their greetings with his head and hand while a faint smile of satisfaction hung from his lips. With his careless conduct today, he might have lost the bricklayer's bows and prostrations for good.

He switched course and began walking in the direction of the bricklayer's house. He must find the bricklayer immediately and demand for his money. But the bricklayer was not likely to be at home. With the kind of pains he came to his house, the bricklayer was not likely to go home. He must have gone straight to Lilong to treat his ulcer. Should he follow the bricklayer to Lilong? But he might not have gone to Lilong. He might have gone to Denkita. There was a hospital there also and the distance to Denkita was about the same with that to Lilong. The best thing was to go and look for the pigs. The pigs were worth far more than the money he gave the bricklayer. He might go chasing the bricklayer without finding him or finding him but without the money only for the pigs to get lost or commit mischief that he would have to pay for. If that happened, he would have lost his trap and the bird the trap was meant to catch. He regained the path leading to the marshy land.

Now again on the way to find the pigs, his mind was more on the pigs than on the money he gave the bricklayer. All his senses were on the lookout for the pigs. It was time they return home and he half-expected to meet them on the way before reaching the marshy land. But he got to the marshy land without meeting the pigs.

At the marshy land, he searched everywhere but did not find the pigs. But he saw two or three stalks of cocoyam that looked like their lumps had recently been eaten. There were also traces of masticated pieces of cocoyam that must have fallen from the mouths of the pigs when they were eating the lumps. He also saw a pond the pigs had rolled in, but did not see the pigs. From the way the mud the pigs smeared on the outer part of the pond had caked, it was clear they left the pond long ago.

Usually when the pigs went to the marshy land, they first nosed about for food before rolling in a pond. After rolling in the mud, they would forage for food again before leaving. From the caking of the mud in the pond, it seemed that was what they did today. From what he could see, the pigs after rolling in the mud began foraging for lumps of cocoyam again and while they were doing so, they were chased away by someone, most likely the owner of the farm. People were becoming very mean he thought. Whoever chased away the pigs did not have the little charity of allowing them eat what they had laboured to find. Whoever chased them away was mean and heartless. It only went to show he must hold tightly to what was his since everyone was holding tight to his own possessions.

Where were the pigs? If rolling in the mud of the pond was the last thing they did before leaving, the mud dripping from their body on the grass would have told him the direction they went, if they left the pond. 'If they left the pond,' he murmured. 'They must have left the pond. No one dares kill my pigs because of miserable lumps of cocoyam they ate in his farm.' All the same, he had to use his eyes more than his ears in his search for the pigs.. There were too many bad people around these days.

He saw a man in his farm of dry maize stalks. Could the man have chased away his pigs or did something worse? He walked to the man and greeted him.

'Ah, Jacob,' said the man. 'Do rich people like you also enter the bush with poor men like us?'

Who does not need the bush Jacob thought angrily? Isn't it from the bush that everyone makes his money? 'We depend on the bush like everyone else to survive,' he said with little interest in what he was saying. His mind was on his pigs.

'You wouldn't know Jacob how tough it is to be poor,' said the man with a moving melancholy that did not reach Jacob. 'When a poor man wears perfume, it smells like kerosene. Even without this famine, everyday a poor man has to wrestle with life to wrest what he will eat. But with the famine, things have moved from bad to worse. Now a barehanded poor man is pitched in battle against life – an enemy that carries a long sword. The locusts left nothing for me. They had no pity for a poor man like me. They ate all that I had in my farms.'

What is this man saying? Jacob wondered. When there is rain, doesn't it fall on everyone's land? And if there were locusts should they ravage only the crops of the rich? he thought angrily.

'I am now in this farm to gather the stalks of corn left behind by the locusts to see if I can find a buyer,' Jacob heard the man saying.

'This is life,' Jacob mumbled. He had come to ask the man of the whereabouts of his pigs, but the man would not even allow him make his inquiry. Instead, he was filling his ears with tales of his own woes. Was he now to abandon the search for his pigs and find food for the man? He was exasperated.

'Have you by any chance seen my pigs around here?' he asked the man, trying unsuccessfully to suppress his exasperation.

'No,' said the man with little interest. He was looking for what to eat while someone had the luxury of looking for pigs that must have eaten more than him. 'I haven't been here for long,' he added, listlessly.

This was the answer Jacob expected. Still it angered him. No one would say he had seen his pigs only to be called again if the pigs were not found or if they were found dead. Everyone you see is out to protect himself. No one is ready to risk himself for the benefit of another. It is a grossly selfish world.

Wherever his pigs were, he had to find and take them home for the days were evil. Searching for the pigs with both his eyes and ears, now and then he stood still, craned his neck and pinned his ears to catch the grunting of the pigs, but would hear nothing. The longer he searched for the pigs, the more his fears increased. Had someone stolen his pigs or killed them?

Moving farther into the marshy land, he met an old man trying to find cocoyam in a harvested farm of cocoyam. 'Have you seen my pigs?' he asked the old man.

'Have I seen your pigs?' the old man repeated Jacob's question, looking vacuous.

'Yes, have you seen my pigs?' Jacob repeated, trying with little success to suppress his rising irritation.

'Did your pigs come here?' the old man asked, rather mechanically.

'Don't be stupid,' Jacob said, unable to control his anger. There were few things he resented like being thrown back a question he had asked or asking someone a question and the person not having the answer begins to ask series of questions that would end up with him telling him he did not know the thing he was asking of. 'If you haven't seen them or seen them and did something evil to them, why not tell me so or hold your peace instead of tormenting me with silly questions?'

'You insult an old man like me!' the old man cried. 'Jacob, I swear it will never be well with you,' he spat, his body shaking with anger and maybe hunger.

'I can see it is well with you,' Jacob said, hissing. He hurriedly walked away from the old man. People who do not wish others well, it will not be well with them, he thought as he walked away. What people don't know is that life is an echo. Everyman's voice comes back to him however long it takes. If it is a good voice, it will come back as a good voice. If a bad voice, it will come back as a bad voice.

Towards the end of the marshy land, he saw a man digging the roots of a tree that were used as a porridge spice. He asked the man the same question he had asked other people before him.

'Pigs, pigs, pigs, which pigs did I see last and where did I see them? Pigs, have I seen any pig today at all?' the man said, speaking more to himself than to Jacob. As he spoke he was rubbing his head with one hand while swinging about him the other hand holding the little hoe he was digging the roots of the tree with. He seemed to be avoiding Jacob's eyes.

What is the meaning of all these theatrics? Jacob wondered. Why was the man avoiding his eyes? Was he trying to hide something? Was there a conspiracy in the bush against him? Had all these people done something evil to his pigs and were now mocking him? He was thoroughly scared. He was so gripped by panic he could not think well. Panic and the fatigue of looking for the pigs were beginning to make him feel sick.

'Jacob, are you well at all? You look sick,' said the man, looking intently at Jacob.

'I am well,' Jacob said, sounding sick. 'But I can't say the same thing about my pigs.'

'Your pigs wherever they are I believe will be well,' said the man, cryptically.

What does he mean by *wherever they are* Jacob wondered. Was there a secret there? If there was, what was it?

'You haven't by any chance seen them?' Jacob asked again with little hope for a positive reply.

'No, I haven't seen them,' the man said with a ring of certainty that contrasted sharply with his earlier uncertain attitudes. His voice and countenance as he spoke seemed to be saying to Jacob, 'I am fed up with you and your inquiries. Get off my back.'

Jacob did not miss the contrast and what the man's voice and face were telling him. His fears for the safety of his pigs deepened. He walked away from the man. He must find the pigs, dead or alive.

Chapter Twelve

From the bush, the bricklayer did not have to listen to hear the noise of the people as they came out of the chief's house. It was so loud he could have heard it much earlier if he had been listening with the same keenness he was when he set out from his house. The crowd was like a moving market. Its noise swallowed the grunting of the pigs completely. But once in a while a pig yelled so loudly that its cry was heard above the din created by the crowd.

The bricklayer wondered if Jacob was in the crowd. He knew it would be pleasing to Bakam's sadism if Jacob and his pigs were paraded around the village for all to see. From Bakam's behaviour, the bricklayer had no doubt he bore the moneylender a grudge well before this unfortunate happening. Well, it is in the nature of men to begrudge those who are prospering. But, he the bricklayer would try not to be like other men. Jacob was a good man. It was those who whispered in the dark against him that were bad. He would not join them in their whispering campaign against such a man. Instead he would do anything to help him and he had already started doing things to help him.

From what he could hear from the crowd, they were going to the earth priest's shrine. The shrine was at one end of the village while the cemetery was at the other. So if they were going to the shrine, they would have to come back the same way to go to the cemetery. So he needn't be in a hurry to place the snake slough beside the road. He could allow the crowd to move completely out of sight before going to place the slough by the roadside. But for one reason he would not do so. He would like to place the slough as close to the earth priest's shrine as possible so that as soon as the crowd comes out of the shrine to go to the cemetery, Bakam would see it and refuse to go to the cemetery with the crowd. That he chickened out as soon as the crowd decides to go to the cemetery to see what he had been claiming would show he had something to hide.

As the crowd moved off from the chief's house, the bricklayer also began to move. The good thing about a crowd is that one can easily move past it unnoticed. It is too involved with itself to notice anyone outside it or indeed to know itself. The crowd has many eyes, but no eye. It has many ears, but no ear. People might have eyes and ears for the crowd, but the crowd has neither eye nor ear for itself or anyone. So the care the bricklayer would have taken if he were trailing an individual, he needed not take against the crowd. However, in movement a crowd is an unpredictable thing. It could suddenly turn away from the shrine and head for the cemetery. So as he followed it, he had to be very watchful of its mood.

The crowd moved on the road, while the bricklayer through the bush – a trailing arbutus without much greens. In the bush, he could feel pain from the ulcer building up from the pit of his stomach. He bit his lips in anguish. The ulcer now seemed to be working for Bakam. Sweat was pouring down his face in torrents. The pain grew so severe that he cried out. Luckily for him the crowd had sufficient noise that absorbed his cry. He quickly retreated deeper into the bush and hide behind a large tree clutching his stomach. The pain from his ulcer showed no sign of abating. Instead it seemed to be increasing. He was now writhing on the ground in severe pains. For sometime he lost consciousness. When he came to, the pain was gone, but there was still sweat on his face. He stood up and listened, but could not hear the noise of the crowd. Had the crowd returned from the earth priest's shrine and walked past him while he was unconscious? He doubted it. It appeared he had not been unconscious long enough for that to have happened.

He set off immediately towards the earth-priest's shrine. As he drew nearer the shrine, he could hear the noise of the people. But it was not as loud as before. Some people must have gone home and the horror of the sacrilege must have begun to lose its initial grip and so people in the shrine were expressing their horror less. But he was sure Bakam was still there. He would be the last to leave.

It was now getting dark. The bricklayer's heart sank. In the darkness of the night Bakam would not see the snake's slough. But the night was also good. If because of it Bakam could not see the slough, because of it the people might not see the ash in Chuwajo's mutilated hand thereby freeing both him and Bakam from suspicion. It was not what he wanted, but it was better than being charged with desecrating Chuwajo's grave – an act considered an attack on the ancestors. Such offence on the dead was worse than one on the living. The reverence accorded the dead was not the reverence accorded the living.

But would the crowd go to the cemetery in the night? It was unlikely. Apart from the problem of not being able observe well the desecration of the grave in the night, night-time was the daytime of the dead when they were full of activity. Everyone in the crowd knew this. To go to the cemetery at night was to court an attack by the spirits of the dead. The spirits of the dead were likely to be more vicious now that the grave of one of them had been desecrated. The Reverend Father or the chief might be irreverent enough to embark on a visit to the cemetery at night, but not the earth priest who knew the full implications.

Since they were not likely to go to the cemetery that night, it was not wise placing the snake slough by the roadside near the earth priest's shrine where Bakam would not see it anyway. Tomorrow morning which now seemed the likely time the earth priest and the people would go to the cemetery, Bakam would set out for the cemetery from his own house and not from the earth priest's shrine. So he should place the snake slough in front of Bakam's house. Bakam would surely see it in the morning when he sets out for the cemetery. Whatever it would cost him, he must avenge himself of Bakam's contempt and shield himself from suspicion over the ash in Chuwajo's grave.

Quickly, he began walking towards Bakam's house. He was impressed with the remarkable care he had handled the snake slough all the while he had it wrapped in the white cloth. Though it had broken in a number of places, it was still largely intact. When he got sufficiently close to the house, he placed the slough beside the path leading to the house and walked hurriedly away.

On his way home, thoughts of treating his ulcer possessed him. Early in the morning tomorrow, he would set out for Lilong Mission Hospital to get treatment for his ailment. Thinking of treating the ulcer, his hand reached for the money in his pocket, but the money was gone. The only thing in the pocket he put the money was the letter of his cousin living in Dawen telling him he was sick and needed help from him.

Chapter Thirteen

At the earth priest's shrine the crowd was more sober than either in the chief's or Reverend Father's house. The earth priest, a one-eyed man was tall and walloping in stature. A burly man with a coarse, humourless face and little charm of manners, he was severe in his demand of proper conduct. His one eye combined with his severe sense of duty made him a frightening man to even those who were used to him. When he spoke, his one eye stood still like a soldier that has submitted to *an order of attention* by his instructor. But it was not the eye that stood to attention that frightened people. It was the missing eye. Though not there, this eye frightened people than the one that was there. If the eye present inspired fear it was not on its own account, but of the missing eye. It was uncanny. But perhaps it was not so uncanny. Ghosts always inspire more fear on the living than people who are alive. His eye standing at attention and his missing eye incapable of movement gave his stare a chilling unity. His one eye was an oracle of some sort and most people feared it more than the shrine.

The shrine was a round building hedged by tall trees with creepers that turned the trees into an outer wall of the shrine. Supplicants to the shrine may on permission by the earth priest go beyond the wall of trees but no supplicant ever went beyond the wall into the shrine. Within the wall of trees there was a line of fresh raffia that no supplicant crossed. It was said the line turned into a snake and wrapped round the neck of a man who once tried to cross it. The man ran out of the shrine with the snake smiting him all over his body. The line, it was also said, once turned to flames of fire around the neck of a man who tried to cross it. Like the first man, this man ran out of the shrine with his necklace of fire. The fire burned the neck to ashes without touching the head or the rest of the man's body. The head fell off his body and rolled to rest at the foot of the shrine like a wedge. To this day the skull of the man's head was still hanging in the shrine. All supplicants to the shrine had heard these stories and whenever they were invited by the earth priest to move beyond the wall of trees, they looked on the line of fresh raffia as a snake or a line of fire. There was no time the raffia leaves that formed the line beyond the wall of trees ever dried. As soon as the raffia leaves began to shrink – an indication they were drying, they were replaced with fresh raffia leaves. Supplicants to the shrine always carried *chemba* – a dry forest fruit with seeds inside which produced a clattering sound when shaken. On getting to the shrine, a supplicant shook the *chemba* to tell the earth priest he was around. The earth priest always sat beyond the line of raffia inside the wall of trees. But when he heard the clattering sound of a supplicant's *chemba*, he emerged from the wall of trees with a calabash half full with earth to know what was the mission of the supplicant to the shrine.

Bakam and his noisy crowd did not need to shake the *chemba* for the earth-priest to emerge from the wall of trees with his calabash half full with earth.

'What brought you to my shrine in such multitude?' asked the earth priest, his one eye already standing at attention.

'Chuwajo's grave has been desecrated,' someone said.

'Who desecrated it?' asked the earth priest with an impassive face.

'Jacob's pigs,' Bakam said. 'After they had eaten what they could, they left the remaining for vultures to devour.'

'This is a sacrilege,' said the earth priest with the same impassive face. 'Where is Jacob?'

'He was not at home when we went to his house. But his brother told us he had gone to look for his pigs.'

'The same pigs that desecrated the grave?'

'Yes, the same pigs.'

'Who saw the pigs desecrating the grave?'

'That is the problem. No one saw them desecrating the graves, but Bakam here saw the footprints of the pigs and their droppings everywhere in the cemetery,' Gochap said.

'This is bad,' said the earth priest, a grim expression replacing the impassive look on his face. 'I can hear the cry of the earth even now that I am standing before you. Pigs exhuming a dead body and allowing vultures to feed on it is taking what belongs to the earth and giving to the sky. Unless this sacrilege is atoned for, we may have to grow our crops in the sky. We cannot deny the earth its due and expect our due from it,' he said in a solemn and haunting voice.

The crowd numbed by a common terror could not speak.

'Our ancestors drew a line for us in the sand which we must never cross,' said the earth priest. 'On the side of the line where we were was where everything good was. On the other side of the line was where everything bad was. But the wind of Christianity and the wind of the quest for material things which had been blowing for a long time now have almost obliterated the line. So young people never saw the line on the sand clearly. Even old people who saw it no longer see it clearly.'

After speaking to the people, the earth priest went into the shrine to perform some rites before coming out to the people again. The people left outside the shrine began speaking among themselves.

'Pigs do not see any line. They burrow everywhere and defecate everywhere. We are all pigs today,' someone said.

'If only this cemetery law was not passed,' another person lamented, absentmindedly.

'Whoever advised the passing of that law must either be a pig, a pig merchant or a vulture,' somebody said.

'How do you seek to please vultures in a law that was supposed to be for the benefit of human beings?' wondered yet another person.

'How do you create different communities for the living and the dead? It is like trying to separate a dog from its newly delivered puppies. We are but puppies of the dead,' said Adubu.

'It is like saying the shadow and the man should live apart. The living are only but the shadows of the dead,' said someone.

'Very soon there will be a law creating a home for the old near the cemetery,' said another person.

'There is already such a law in England,' said Adubu.

'The old and the dead will then be burying themselves.'

'But the dead should be able to take care of themselves if they take care of the living,' someone said, cynically.

'That is blasphemy. Be careful man!' another person cried.

'You know the government has lost its head,' said Gochap. 'There is now a law that says no one should harvest honey with fire. I wonder how we are supposed to harvest our honey now that the government is more interested in pleasing bees than people. You set up your big pot on a tree and honey bees take it over without you being able to extract rent from them by taking honey from the pot once in a while. How can you take honey from a honey pot without fire? Man is counting less and less to his fellow man. The wind has changed direction. Very soon we may have to go to the animals for favours.'

'Gochap, maybe you are right about the wind changing direction,' said someone. 'But who cares about the direction of any wind? Any wind for that matter is not good.'

'That is not true,' said another person. 'The wind that brings rain is good. Before bringing rain, it is the wind that impregnates the sky to deliver rain.'

'That is not true. It is water from the earth that impregnates the sky. It is the same water that returns in the form of rain to impregnate the earth. The wind has no role in it,' somebody said.

'Even if it is the wind that impregnates the sky, the wind the earth priest is talking about will make the earth barren. What is the usefulness of a fertile sky without a fertile earth?' said Bakam.

At this point, the earth priest came out of the shrine again and a hush immediately fell on the crowd.

'Earth priest,' said Gochap, bending in obeisance, 'what of the line of fire in your shrine? I believe we have not crossed it.'

'You will never get round to crossing that line without paying for it with your head,' said the earth priest with a clear threat in his voice. 'So the line in my shrine is not the line of concern. The line of concern is the line our ancestors drew for us in the sand. This line was drawn everywhere including the shrine. It is the line that has been blurred by the wind. It is the line we are crossing to our sorrow.'

"What do we do now?' Adubu asked.

'Tomorrow after we have gone to the cemetery and seen its desecration, Bosuu will tell us what to do to appease the earth,' said the earth priest.

Chapter Fourteen

For a very long time, Jacob searched for his pigs. When he could not find them in the marshy land, he went to Tasso plains where he also knew they used to wander to. Tasso plains were largely rice growing stretches of land that started from the road to Lilong and ended by a little stream that fed river Patei. There was hardly any pig food in these plains and Jacob often wondered what attracted the pigs to the plains. In the end, he observed that the pigs often went to the plains after they had eaten their fill. So they went to there not to find food but to refresh themselves.

The pigs were not in the plains when he got there. He made his way through a thicket of small trees and big shrubs to see if the pigs might be lying inside the thicket, but did not see any pig. Feeling tired and despondent, he sat down on a boulder near the thicket to rest for a while before continuing the search. While sitting on the boulder, he saw a woman returning from the forest with firewood on her head. Coming from the forest as she was he did not see the point of asking her whether she had seen his pigs, but seeing no one else in the plains to inquire after the pigs, he asked her.

'Since morning I have been in the forest,' said the woman, pausing in her walk and turning to face Jacob. Standing with the heap of firewood on her head, she kept heaving the wooden carrier the firewood was stacked. This was done to relieve her smitten skull by finding a less painful position on her head to rest the load. 'I have not seen your pigs,' she continued in a tone that sounded friendly to Jacob. 'Pigs and dogs give the same headache. They would wander far away and the owner would have to go in search of them. That is where the cat is better.' Talking with a heavy load on the head was a very stressful thing and the stress on the woman's face as she spoke was very visible.

'Thank you,' said Jacob, his mind now with a herdsman passing by with his herd of cattle. Like all herdsmen, this one looked thin. As a nomad, a herdsman keeps his possessions low so that they don't hamper his movements, Jacob thought with pity in his heart. Having little flesh on his body is part of the necessity of having less to carry along on the treacherous forest paths the herdsman traverses year round. But while he wants to have little flesh on his body, he wants a lot of flesh on his cows which often have the additional burden of carrying his personal effects when he moves camp.

Like with the woman, Jacob knew there was little hope finding from the herdsman where his pigs were. But in addition to looking with his eyes for the pigs and listening with his ears to hear their grunts, he had to ask whoever he came across whether he had seen the pigs. The look on the herdsman's face when he asked him whether he had seen his pigs was like he had asked him if he had seen the devil. His words and attitude expressed more eloquently the feelings that had reported on his face.

'Pigs,' intoned the herdsman. 'Those scandalous creatures?'

Jacob was incensed, but controlled his anger. Who told this rude wanderer that cows were not scandalous? What of the herdsman? Was he not a scandal himself? With his stick and the rags he had on him, he was more than a scandal.

'Please, have you by any chance seen them?' he asked the herdsman again.

'I don't eat pigs and I don't know anybody who eats them.'

How better off he would have been if he were eating pigs, Jacob thought. He would have had more flesh on his ragged body and wouldn't have been the skeleton he was.

'Is it only things you eat that you see?'

'I hate them.'

'Is it only things you love that you see?'

'Well, I haven't seen your pigs and I am happy I haven't seen them,' replied the herdsman, curtly. 'Pigs, why should I see them? Of what use are they? In fact I wish not to see them. All the problems of this world are caused by pigs. Even this famine I suspect pigs are behind it. It was a pig that deceived Adam and Eve, not the serpent. I wonder what the world would have been like if there were as many pigs as cows in it. Even with the few pigs around, look at what they have brought the world to. The world would be a peaceful place, and I believe a cleaner place, without pigs.'

Jacob was deeply depressed. With the exception of the woman, all the people he had inquired after his pigs from had behaved as if he was asking after some leprous and worthless creatures. It was infuriating. With this kind of attitude, people around here would never be rich. He stood up from the boulder and began walking away from the plains.

Where could these pigs be? he wondered. Well, he would not return home until he found them. His brother was at home taking care of the pig that had just delivered and its piglets. He should find the pigs that had strayed away from home and take care of them.

From the plains, he wandered through a piece of fallow bush-land. Beneath a big shrub he saw a hole he suspected must be that of a bandicoot rat. As a child, he and his age mates always went to the bush to hunt for bandicoot rats and so he was very familiar with bandicoot rat holes. Of all rodents, the bandicoot rat is the one that most behaves like the pig, he thought. There is hardly anything the bandicoot rat does not eat. Inside its hole are to be found assorted food items. When digging a hole in search of a bandicoot rat, the first thing that told him and his friends the rodent was in the hole was the presence of bits of dry grasses, groundnut seeds and pods, bits of yam, grains of corn or pieces of dry meat. The more of these things they found as they dug deeper, the more the chances were there was a bandicoot rat in the hole.

Sometimes after a bandicoot rat dug a hole, a ground snake would chase it away and take over the hole. So if they did not see any of these food items in the hole that was apparently dug by a bandicoot rat, it was likely a ground snake had chased away the bandicoot rat and now lived in the hole.

Digging for bandicoot rats particularly in the dry season was a back-breaking labour. Bandicoot rat holes were always very deep. When digging the hole he and his friends always wanted to know how far they still had to dig before getting to the rodent which upon the commencement of digging would retreat deeper into the hole. So now and then the person digging extended his hand into the hole to feel the extent of the hole and maybe sense the presence of the rodent. But because of the possibility of a snake in the hole, an experienced bandicoot rat hunter never stuck his hand into the hole but instead used sticks to rifle the hole to locate the bandicoot rat. If it was not a bandicoot rat but a snake it could only smite the stick. Even if it was a bandicoot rat, it could only bite the stick. When a hole was properly riffled, a bandicoot rat would run out of the hole if there was nowhere to hide inside. If it ran out, they would chase it with their sticks and club it to death. But if a bandicoot rat was stubborn and there was somewhere to hide in the hole, it took them more than rifling its hole to smoke out the rodent. For such bandicoot rat, water if nearby, had to be fetched and poured into the hole. This often forced the bandicoot rat out of the hole on the run. But it was always wise to leave one of their numbers by the hole while going to fetch the water or to block the hole with a stone if there was no one to guard it. One day, he and his two friends failed to take any of these precautionary measures, but instead they all went to fetch the water. Before they returned from the stream with the water, the bandicoot rat had escaped from the hole.

Now he could also call to mind a funny incident in his adolescence when he and a friend went to hunt for bandicoot rats. The friend was better than him in knowing which hole there was a bandicoot rat. His friend was such a good bandicoot rat hunter that he could even tell the size of a bandicoot rat by the size of the hole and the food items they were turning up while digging the hole. That day they found a hole his friend said a bandicoot rat was definitely inside. And sure when they started digging, they began turning up bandicoot rat food items – an indication the game was inside the hole. Surprisingly, his friend started showing lack of interest in digging the hole further saying there was no bandicoot rat in the hole and so they should go home. He protested pointing to the various food items they had already turned up, but his friend insisted there was no bandicoot rat in the hole.

'What I can smell in this hole is the odour of a big ground snake,' said the friend, picking his hoe and walking away from the hole.

'But look at the grains of millet and bits of grasses that we have turned up,' he said still standing by the hole.

'Forget about all those things,' said the friend, exhaling a stream of hot air through his nostrils. 'I believe the snake just chased out the bandicoot rat that is why you can still find those food items in the hole. Jacob; no, what I smell is bad.'

The way his friend spoke only helped to fuel his suspicion about his motive and real reason of abandoning the hole; so he decided to play along like a fool and followed his friend back home. As soon as they got home, he saw his friend going back to the bush and he followed him at a distance. His friend went back to the hole and began digging it for the bandicoot rat. He climbed a tree not far from where his friend was digging and waited. Not long after, he heard the squealing of a bandicoot rat and saw it in the hands of his friend who had caught it. He jumped down from the tree. His friend was shocked and embarrassed to see him.

'I had a rethink about this hole; that was why I returned,' he said, avoiding his eyes.

'I also had a rethink about it and that was why I too returned,' he said and laughed. His friend had no choice but share the bandicoot rat with him.

Now he walked to the bandicoot rat hole he had seen and peeped inside. There was no doubt there was a bandicoot rat inside the hole. 'Bandicoot rat, where are my pigs?' he murmured, sorrowfully.'

It was surprising that at a time of hunger like this, a bandicoot rat hole not very far from the village was yet to be dug by someone looking for food. He brought some dry grasses and stalks of corn to cover the opening of the hole. When he finds his pigs, he would return to the hole with a hoe.

He walked past the bandicoot rat hole further into a fallow land. A squirrel, probably dead from hunger, lay in the sun like an open sore that had dried. Even flies were not going near it because there was nothing for them to pick. The whole scene told a silent story of misery and death. He shook his head and moved on. The famine was beginning to chime like boiling water in a big ceremonial pot, he thought. Beyond the fallow bush-land, he came to a farm corn was grown the previous year. In about two places in the farm, he saw a sheaf of corn that had survived the locusts and escaped the eyes of the farmer after the locusts. There was hunger; yet sheaves of corn were lying in the sun eaten by the sun and the wind, he thought. Maybe the hunger was not as bad as he thought. Maybe people were becoming more careless and lazy than he thought. Else, how could the owner of this farm leave so many sheaves of corn behind and nobody has picked what he left behind?

Night was now falling and still there was no sign of his pigs. His desperation was fast giving way to panic. What had happened to his pigs? Would he ever find them?

Beyond the farm of corn, he saw the droppings of a pig. His heart jumped in excitement. He moved closer to the droppings and saw further droppings ahead of him. He began walking hurriedly following the direction of the droppings towards the cemetery.

Chapter Fifteen

In utter desperation and panic the bricklayer searched all the pockets of his shirt and trousers, but did not find the money. He took off his clothes, shook and tossed them about, but no money fell out. He felt faint. It was like he was going to have a heart attack. How could he lose this money on which his life now hung? Where could he have lost it among the many places he had gone to since it was given to him? When last did he feel the money in his pocket? He tried to remember, but it was difficult to remember. It was not that he had not been touching the pocket he put the money to feel it. He had been touching the pocket and feeling the money. But it now seemed it was the letter he had been feeling thinking it was the money. Being voluminous, it seemed it was the letter that forced the money out of his pocket. He was so furious that he tore the letter and threw the pieces into the darkness with a curse. Why is it that useless things hardly get lost? he wondered angrily. Whenever you are looking for something useful, you hardly find it. But you would keep seeing useless things you don't need. For days he had carried the letter with him without it getting lost. But just a while ago he was given money and it was lost. And the letter was to blame for the loss of the money. If it were not in his pocket to push out the money and deceive him, the money wouldn't have fallen out of his pocket and if it did, he would have long discovered the loss and looked for it. He could not explain why he had carried the letter with him all this while. Could he be under some diabolical influence? A letter asking him for help over the sickness of someone who had never helped him was now threatening his own life. It was so annoying. Could his cousin by some magic have taken away his money to cure himself leaving him to death? He was bewildered by the inexplicable.

He could not think clearly because fear was clogging his brain. He felt too weak to walk, so he sat down on a small anthill he could see by the moonlight. He began to cry. He would die of his ulcer if he did not find the money. After crying for a while, he stood up and began walking to the cemetery to look for the money. Maybe that was where it fell off his pocket. Crying would not help him. It was better he went and looked for the money in all the places he had gone to, particularly the places he had a lot of activity. The cemetery was the place he had a lot of activity. *But could he afford to go to the cemetery at night when all the dead were out and about? What does it matter?* he thought. He would die if he did not find the money. He might as well go to the cemetery and die there. What does it matter?

He had no torch; but the moon was shining, not very bright, but bright enough for him to see the money if he got sufficiently close to it. Even in the desperate state he found himself, he still took care he met no one on his way to the cemetery. So he still walked in the bush instead of the road. Now he was a moving shadow with less fear of being seen and recognised from afar. But he had to be wary of snakes. The fear of death was an uncanny thing. Though he had told himself he might as well die in the cemetery, he was careful not to be bitten by a snake. Like it was for ghosts, night time was the time for snakes movement and in the treacherous bush full of dry elephant grass, stepping on a snake was an ever possibility.

Near the cemetery, he saw a figure moving away from the graveyard. It was Jacob hurrying back home though he had not found his pigs. Maybe they had since gone back home while he had been searching for them everywhere in the bush. But his brother should have come to tell him instead of allowing him wallow in the bush this long. This life; not even your brother can carry your firewood for you. But with whom would his brother leave the pigs and piglets at home? Surely his wife must have returned by now. She could not possibly be in the market alone, no matter how much she loved it. Even the mad woman that always sat with her rags by the roadside in front of the market would have left the market now for her shack under the mango tree. But how would his brother have found him even if he had looked for him? He had been looking for the pigs everywhere. All the same, his brother ought to have looked for him. But had the pigs gone home? That was what he had to hurry home to find out.

Perhaps because the bricklayer was in deep thought he did not see the figure of Jacob as early as he would have if he were less engrossed in his thoughts. The suddenness with which the figure sprung up and the fact that he was already afraid before it materialized from nowhere made him lame with fear. It was like part of the night had collected into the figure which was now walking through the shadow that produced it. He stopped walking and watched the figure drifting away into the abyss of the night. Who could it be? he wondered. This is the problem with the night. It reduces all human beings to creeping shadows. When night falls and the shadow of a man goes to sleep, it is the man that becomes a shadow. Had the figure seen him? It was unlikely. It had just sprung up and walked away without pausing or appearing to peer too closely into the darkness. After the figure had disappeared in the fog of the night, the bricklayer began walking again towards the cemetery. He has to be more watchful he told himself. This one was too close.

When he got to the cemetery, he searched everywhere for the money, but did not find it. But his mind kept telling him it was in the cemetery the money fell off his pocket. He looked up the tree where the vultures were perching in the daytime. Were they still there looking down at him as he searched the cemetery for the money? Did they carry the money? A vulture was never to be trusted. They might peck it thinking it was decaying human flesh.

No, it could not have been the vultures that picked the money. It must be a human being. Which human being could have picked the money? His mind went back to the figure he saw walking away. Who was it? Was it Chuwajo's ghost? If it was his ghost, where was it going? Did it carry his money to punish him for what he did? He was so frightened he stopped the search and began to walk quickly away from the cemetery.

He went back to where he had fainted and searched for the money, but found nothing. Could it be that when he fainted someone came and removed the money from his pocket? It was a cruel, unsympathetic world full of vultures without pity. Dead to the world as he was, someone could remove the money from his pocket and walk away without thinking of his condition. But was that what happened or did Jacob give him ghost money which could be recalled by the giver? He had heard about such money several times. It was said not to stay with whoever it was given to, but returned to the original owner. That must be the type of money Jacob gave him. How could a miser like Jacob pay him his money and even give him two hundred bembo for free unless it was ghost money? But was it ghost money or real money that fell on the road after he left Jacob's house and someone picked it? Could Bakam the first person he met after leaving Jacob's house have picked it? Or did Bakam have a magic wand that made the money disappear from his pocket into Bakam's pocket? Bakam had asked if Jacob had given him money. How did he know this if he was not a money-pinching magician? He went to Bakam's house where he left the snake slough, but the money was not there also. A cock crowed and he began to hurry home.

At home, he searched everywhere for the money, but did not find it. His ulcer which had died down was beginning to bite him again.

Chapter Sixteen

Bakam left his house early the following morning to go to the earth priest's shrine so that he and other people could go to the cemetery and see how Jacob's pigs had desecrated Chuwajo's grave. The first thing he saw when he came out of his house was a snake slough. The moment he saw the slough, a startled look replaced the hitherto carefree expression on his face. What was the meaning of this? He had no doubt it was the previous night the snake left behind the slough because he did not see it the day before. Besides, the slough looked new though it was broken in a number of places. Well, now there was no way he could go to the earth priest's shrine and the cemetery. Though it was morning, he was sweating. He turned and walked back into his house.

At the shrine, the earth priest, the chief and the people including Jacob waited for Bakam to lead them to the cemetery, but Bakam did not turn up. Tired of waiting someone was sent to his house to see what was keeping him at home, but Bakam had told his wife to tell anyone that came to look for him that he was not at home.

'How could a man who came here fuming and swearing at Jacob yesterday be nowhere to be found today when we want to go and confirm his allegation?' wondered the earth priest.

'You know how some people are,' said somebody. 'He was all courage and anger yesterday because Jacob was not around. Now that Jacob is around I believe all his courage has forsaken him.'

'Some dreams appear great in the night, but in the morning they seem emptied of all their promise of greatness,' said someone.

'In fact in the morning you forget most dreams,' said another person.

The earth priest, the chief and the people including Jacob decided to go to the cemetery without Bakam. The people spoke less on the way to the cemetery largely because everyone was trying to keep pace with the earth priest. The earth priest was always on the wings of the wind. Tall and walloping, he took long, sweeping strides that to him might not be walking fast, but which made others run to keep pace with him. By the time they got to the cemetery, most people were sweating and panting.

Four vultures were in the cemetery when they got there. Three of the vultures were on the ground while the fourth was on top of the tree. What looked like a tear of human flesh hung from the beak of one of the vultures on the ground. It was lowering it towards its claws probably to hold it with its talons so as to be able to cut it to pieces its mouth could handle. The vulture on the tree looked down at the vultures on the ground with what seemed an expression of lethargy and boredom. It seemed to think it was too early to eat and was not sparing understanding for the vultures that were eating so early. The vultures on the ground did not immediately fly away on seeing the earth priest and the people. They only flew up the tree when they drew very close to where they were.

For a while, the attention of the earth priest, the chief and the people was more on the vultures on top of the tree than on the cemetery. The vultures were looking at them with an air of indifference that bothered on insolence. The vultures looked like prosperous predators while the people looked like famished preys.

The people with the earth priest and the chief could not stand the haughty graces of the vultures on top of the tree. They started hurling stones at them.

'Stop it,' said the earth priest. 'What is the matter with you? Never throw stones at a vulture that sees you but refuses to fly away. There is always more to such a vulture than what you can see.'

The people stopped throwing stones at the vultures, but it was of no use. All the vultures had flown away.

'Kash,' muttered the earth priest watching the vultures fly away.

'What is this?' the chief looking at the cemetery exclaimed. His exclamation made the earth priest who had been looking at the fleeing vultures to look down at the cemetery. If he was shocked by what he saw, his face did not show it. The cemetery looked like a legion of carrion-eaters held a party on it the previous night. Paws and hoofs had turned the cemetery into a big dusty bowl of small ditches and round ridges. There were more pawprints than hoofprints. The pawprintss were clearly those of hyenas while the few hoofprints could not be said to be clearly those of pigs. Hyenas were common in Tounga probably because the area was full of rocks and caves. The hyenas lived mostly in the caves in the daytime, but at night went out to hunt for food. When they could not find a sheep or goat, they fed on any carrion they could find.

Since the cemetery was created, there had been no incident of hyenas desecrating a grave. So what the people were seeing was as alarming as it was shocking. For a while they stood looking at the defiled cemetery in shock and alarm. This was not what they came to the cemetery to see. Yesterday Bakam told them it was Chuwajo's grave that was desecrated. But now it looked like the whole cemetery had been desecrated. Three other graves were desecrated even more than Chuwajo's. What was the meaning of these? What was happening? Has the famine declared war on the dead after declaring it on the living?

'We thought it was only Chuwajo's grave that Jacob's pigs and the vultures had desecrated,' somebody said. 'What are we seeing? The whole cemetery has been desecrated and not only by pigs and vultures, but by hyenas as well. This is terrible!'

The earth priest first went and inspected Chuwajo's grave. Almost the whole corpse had been exhumed. Most of the flesh of the dead body had been eaten. The flesh that had not been eaten had been hideously mutilated. While the flesh on one hand was completely gone, there was a deep cut on the hand still having flesh. From the neatness and sharpness of the cut, it was clear it could not have been made by the teeth of a predator or its talons. It was the cut of a knife. The ashy substance where the cut was made further convinced him the cut was made by a human agency. 'Something very bad has happened here,' he said.

Indeed,' said many voices together.

'Go closer and see what I have seen,' the earth priest said, leaving the grave and going to a bammo tree not far from the cemetery to perform rites of divination.

With hands over their mouths and noses, the people moved to the grave to have a closer look at the desecration. But the sight and stench of the corpse soon made them to move far away from it again.

'What do you think is the ashy substance in the dead body?' someone asked after they had retreated from the corpse.

Some people said it was ash while others said it was gunpowder.

'But I couldn't perceive the smell of gunpowder,' someone said.

'How could you perceive the smell of gunpowder in a decomposing body?' asked Gochap. 'When a skunk is passing by cow dung how do you start talking of the smell of the cow dung? The footprint of the elephant has covered that of the camel and so no one can see the footprint of the camel.'

'That is not gunpowder,' another person said. 'Water and ogogoro may look the same, but they don't have the same taste. Ash and gunpowder may look alike, but they don't have the same smell. The smell I perceived there was that of ash not gunpowder.'

'You must have the nose of a rat to perceive the smell of ash in a decomposing body,' said Adubu. 'But even if it is ash, someone must have poured it where the cut is.'

'This is terrible!' someone exclaimed.

'Whoever did this, the locusts left with his heart,' said Gochap.

'Since the locusts attack, cases of theft and barbaric conduct have increased,' said someone.

'You have said something there,' said Gochap. 'Locusts come to steal and plunder. I suspect when locusts attack they create a thieving tendency in the people they leave behind. The people begin to behave like the locusts. Locusts like barbarians leave behind a culture of looting.'

'Our government behaves like locusts,' someone said. 'Like locusts, our government has no mercy.'

'The locusts left behind *A Eat All* mentality,' Adubu said. 'So corpses are now being eaten.'

'We ought to have treated the government like locusts. To eat it after it has eaten us,' somebody said.

'You ate the locusts that perched where you could reach,' said Adubu. 'Those that perched high up the trees no one ate them. It is the same thing with the government. You cannot eat the government. The government is an eagle on a tall tree beyond your reach.'

'That is what you think,' said a young man behind Adubu. 'If I wanted to eat the locusts that perched high on a tree I would have carried an axe and fell the tree. It is the same thing with the government. If we mean to eat this government, we can all take our machetes and axes and fell the tall tree you said it is perching on.'

'You speak according to your age,' said Adubu, turning to look at the young man that had just spoken. 'At your age, there is nothing the axe or machete cannot cut. But when you grow to my age, you will find that there are many things the axe or machete cannot cut. It is like the tortoise; he thought there was no one he could not trick until he met the hare.'

'It is old men like you that make us fear the fear that fears us,' said the young man with a lot of anger.

'Ayuk, what do you mean by *a fear that fears us*?' someone asked.

'I mean government fears us; so it is a fear,' said Ayuk. 'It is absurd that we fear what fears us. You old men would say you saw yesterday, but will not tell us you learned little from what you saw yesterday.'

'Ayuk, though you are a rash young man, I think you have said something there,' said an elderly man. 'I cannot deny a mad man what he has said that is right just because he is a mad man. We ought not to fear the teeth the government bares at us. Government is like the hyena. It fears you even as it charges at you.'

'We are beginning to think well.'

'And talk well, you forgot to add.'

'Even for a locust mentality, it is terrible to loot the cemetery,' concern predictably veered towards the locusts.

'I think we are allowing our imagination to run wild,' said Watto. 'The desperation we find ourselves is pushing us and the animals to do these terrible things. It is not anything left behind by the locusts.'

'Watto, what are you saying?' somebody asked. 'Is it the first time we are going through a famine? Five years ago there was famine as a result of drought, who saw anything near what we are seeing today? I believe the locusts even left some of them with us. They are the ones obliterating the line our ancestors drew in the dust.'

Chapter Seventeen

As if by a spell, for a long while no one in the cemetery spoke. Everyone seemed in a trance of deep thought. When the spell broke, almost at once everyone began to talk of who or what he thought must have desecrated Chuwajo's grave and the other graves in the cemetery.

'It must be a hunter that did this. It is only hunters that have gunpowder.'

'Bakam is the only hunter in Tounga; at least the only hunter with a gun and gunpowder.'

'It doesn't have to be a hunter. Anyone can buy gunpowder in the market.'

'But buy it to do what?'

'A muscle has been cut from Chuwajo's hand near the wrist. Clearly, it must have been cut for a charm. Hunters are always after one charm or the other.'

'It must be Bakam that did this. That is why he is not here. What treachery? To desecrate Chuwajo's grave only to accuse my pigs. What treachery!'

'When the fowl fouls the ground with its faeces, the earth gives it a chase. So it runs from its excreta.'

'Maybe he thought the village would not come to the cemetery to check his allegations.'

'When he found that the village was coming to the cemetery, he ran away.'

'That was why when the chief said we should not come to the cemetery yesterday he was the first person to support him.'

'But if he did what we suspect him of, why should he be the one to report himself by screaming over the sacrilege the way he did?'

'You are asking this question because you don't know the tricks of the tortoise. The tortoise, to ward off suspicion from himself, after stealing groundnut from the farm of the rabbit, was the first animal to report the theft to the lion. Bakam is a tortoise.'

'If he knew he had done what we are saying he did, he would have preferred that we come to the cemetery at night when we might not easily see the gunpowder.'

'Like any of us, he fears the ghosts. So he would not want to come to the cemetery at night, especially knowing what he had done.'

'That is one thing,' said Adubu. 'Another thing is that he could have hoped that something might happen in the course of the night to reduce or even remove any suspicion of misdeed against him, and something had happened in the night.'

'Could Bakam have sent the hyenas?' someone wondered aloud. 'You know he is a hunter. He could trick the hyenas to the cemetery.'

'If he did so, he would have been in the cemetery now, knowing he had nothing to fear. Let's be reasonable,' some other person said.

'No, Bakam could not have brought the hyenas to the cemetery. We need to look deeper into this matter. There is more to it than meets the eye,' another person said.

'Maybe the pigs first desecrated Chuwajo's grave. Bakam came and saw his chance and took it,' somebody said. 'The vultures and hyenas also came later and saw their chances and took them. Life is about exploiting opportunities.'

'Maybe Bakam first opened Chuwajo's grave. The pigs came and met him and he ran off to the village to report them. That way he frees himself of blame and passes it to the pigs,' said another person.

'Maybe after opening the grave and doing what he did, he saw the pigs passing by the cemetery and lured them to Chuwajo's grave,' somebody said.

'How could he have lured them to the grave?' someone asked.

'If he left the grave open, the smell from the open grave would lure the pigs to the grave. How many times would you be excreting in the bush and the stench from your excreta would draw pigs from far and near. Pigs are like flies,' said Adubu.

'But if Bakam did what we are accusing him, why should he leave such damning evidence as his gunpowder behind in the hand of the dead man?' Gochap asked.

'Maybe he had to do that for the charm he wants to use the muscle for to work,' somebody replied. Other people went on to talk according to what they thought and felt.

'Whoever did this, the earth saw him.'

'So did the vultures.'

'But the vultures only came later. They couldn't have seen the person.'

'You don't know vultures. They are like bats. They see in the dark.'

'The earth must be appeased. Maybe it was this kind of sacrilege that brought the locusts.'

'The village has been reduced to a carcass and Jacob is the vulture feasting on it,' somebody said, steering lamentation towards Jacob.

'If people have no food, they go to buy it from him.'

'Rumour has it he has been persuading his brother to become a coffin-maker so that when we die of hunger, we will buy our coffins from him.'

'Such a man.'

He is a template of opportunism that inspires self-seeking in others.'

He is the tabernacle that does not carry the Ark of the Covenant but the Ark of shame.'

'Now that his brother is not yet a coffin-maker, those of us who die and are not buried in a coffin, he sends his pigs to feed on them. That which the locusts could not eat, the pigs would eat.'

'I have never known a more fortunate man in my life.'

'But why are we talking as if Jacob is alone in his opportunism? As far as I know, we are all opportunists in this country. During Christmas and Sallah festivals market women and traders raise the prices of their commodities without pity for anyone.'

'Even the government is opportunistic. It is taking advantage of the ignorance and docility of our people to steal our money, ripping the people off without the rebuke of their consciences – that is if people in government in this country have conscience.'

'Well, you don't blame the government. We are so docile.'

'You are right there. I have heard someone said that the Minister of Culture and Tourism said the masses of this country would have to suffer to the full extent of their docility.'

'You are all right including the minister. But what we are saying is that the opportunism of Jacob keeps yawning even as he swallows all that we have.'

'Whatever evil befell this cemetery Jacob's pigs started it,' said the chief, breaking his long thoughtful silence.

'That was what Bakam said and he is not here,' someone said.

'But we can see the footprints of the pigs and their droppings,' said another person.

'We can also see Bakam's gunpowder,' some other person said.

'The hare does not always blame the person who killed it as the person who caused it to leave its lair. So I believe Chuwajo's ghost and the ghosts of the other dead people whose graves have been desecrated must be angrier with Jacob,' said the chief. But it is not only with Jacob they are angry. They are angry with everyone.'

'If that is true, we are in more trouble than the one the locusts threw at us,' someone said in a voice full of alarm.

'You remember what I said yesterday evening when some of you wanted us to come to the cemetery at night to see the desecration of Chuwajo's grave,' said the chief with an air of royalty that was as unbecoming as a crown on a donkey's head. 'I said then it would be dangerous and unwise to do so seeing that the spirits of the dead would be out in the night for vengeance after the desecration of the grave of one of them. Now more graves have been desecrated. From what I can see in this cemetery, we are now pitched in battle against the dead, and who can fight a spirit? No one expects the spirits of the dead men whose graves and bodies had been desecrated to still be in their desecrated bodies. They are now abroad as vengeful ghosts ready to strike. For the next two weeks, I can see different ghosts wandering about the village terrorising people that venture out of their homes. Because ghosts do not eat food, at least our type of food, Chuwajo's ghost and the ghosts of the other dead men will not understand why we have to leave our houses to find food for our stomachs. So for these two weeks that we will have to remain indoors, Jacob would have to feed us. For me, Jacob you know I take every meal with a lot of meat. If Jacob fails to feed the village for the two weeks I have decreed, anyone may go to his house and take what he finds to feed himself. The day the thorny creeper strays into the path is the day its ears are cut. Jacob, you have strayed into our path and that is why your ears would be cut.'

For a long while both Jacob and his brother were so stunned by the absurdity of what the chief had said and his judgment that they could not say anything. However, other people began to talk immediately after the chief had finished speaking.

'But it was not Jacob's pigs that desecrated the other graves,' somebody protested. 'Why should Jacob be punished alone?'

'Who was that?' asked the chief, looking with facile anger in the direction of the man who had spoken.

Some quiet fell on the crowd.

'His pigs may not be alone in the desecration of the cemetery,' said the chief, 'but they started the whole thing. If they had not desecrated Chuwajo's grave, the hyenas and the vultures wouldn't have been drawn to the cemetery by the stench of the decomposing body. It was when the hyenas and vultures were drawn to the cemetery by the smell of the decomposing body that they desecrated the other graves. Besides, as we all know, a hare does not blame the person that eventually kills it, but the person who forced it out of its lair.'

As soon as the chief finished talking, he left the cemetery.

'This is an opportunistic decision,' someone murmured as the chief was leaving. 'If the dead are up in arms, why didn't they kill the hyenas and the vultures that came in the night to desecrate other graves or are they looking for only human beings? Why have they not descended on us all the while we have been here?'

'The times are opportunistic times,' murmured the man standing near the man who first murmured.

'I am beginning to see the chief as chief,' someone said. Other people talked as they were led by their thoughts:

'This decision couldn't have come at a better time.'

'The chief is beginning to make amends for his previous misdeeds.'

'If the chief continues along this line, he will surely get somewhere.'

'Now is the time for Jacob to vomit what he has stolen from us.'

'This is a heavy tax.'

'Jacob's pigs would have to help him pay it.'

'His pigs might make the sky to withhold the tax we expect from it in the form of rain.'

'Talking about rain reminds me of the story of the foolish farmer that nailed his ears against the warnings of an imminent rain in his blind commitment to get wealth from the soil,' said Adubu. 'The rain winked at the foolish farmer by way of lightning, but he did not see. By thunder, the rain shouted at him, but he did not hear. It began to pinch him by drizzles; but he refused to feel the pinch. So the rain with big ice blocks came down heavily upon the farmer and thrashed him mercilessly. Jacob is a man whose love for wealth hearkens to no warning.'

'Jacob, what opportunists like you don't know is that after you finish taking advantage of opportunities, you will be an opportunity others will take advantage of,' said Gochap. 'When you treat people unfairly, you can only expect to be treated unfairly in the end. When Jacob treated Esau unfairly, he received his *just deserts* from Laban the father of Rachel. Laban seeing that Jacob loved his beautiful daughter Rachel promised to give her in marriage to him if he would serve him for seven years. Jacob served him for the seven years, but after the seven years, Laban seeing how desperate Jacob wanted to have Rachel as wife asked him to serve him for another seven years before he could give him Rachel as wife. Jacob had no choice but to serve Laban for another seven years and ended up marrying an old maid instead of the maiden he originally set out to marry. That is how opportunists often end up.'

Everyone started talking at once in a free-for-all banter.

'Jacob has the heart of a vulture...'

'A heart that preys on the misfortunes of others without pity.'

'Jacob is the unknown vulture that feasted on the cemetery ...'

'A rapacious and heartless beast.'

'He is the unknown vulture we live with in the village ...'

'He is never faraway when misfortune is lighting upon us.'

'But let the person who breaches trust know that after breaching all the trust in the world, his own trust will be breached. And let the person who spoils others know that after spoiling others, he would be spoiled.'

'It is not good for a camel that chances upon an oasis to drink all the water of the oasis. If the poor and thirsty lives of the desert cannot find water to drink, they might be forced to cut open the stomach of the camel for a drink.'

'When an elder takes what belongs to a child, he would have to hand it over to the child when his hand begins to ache,' said Adubu who had not spoken for a while.

'Jacob has not been paying his taxes to the chief that was why he was so eager to pass judgment on him,' said someone.

'That is not true,' another person said. 'The chief passed his funny judgment because he has the heart of Jacob.'

'It is not only the chief that has the heart of Jacob,' said yet another person. 'We all have the heart of Jacob. We are all vultures and that is why we are all happy with the chief's judgment.'

'Jacob has wronged both God and the devil?' said another person.

'How is that possible?' someone asked

'A man who in the beginning professed to be an upright man of truth following the path of God but who later leaves his path for that of the devil by supporting lies and evil has wronged both God and the devil,' another person replied.

'How?'

'He wronged the devil when he was with God and God now that he is with the devil.'

'There is no evil like wronging both God and the devil. It is like a woman insulting both her mother and father in-law.'

'There is no refuge for such a woman.'

'But I have not seen much of Jacob's pigs footprints here or their droppings,' said someone

'You have food in your house that is why you can't see them,' said another person. 'For me I can see evidences of the pigs having been here all over the place. Yes, I can see around me the carnage wrought by hyenas and vultures. I can see signs of a human being scooping the loose soil with his bare hands. But I can also see the burrowing of the ground by pigs everywhere. The burrowing by pigs is different from hyenas scratching the earth or human beings scooping it with their hands.'

'That is not true,' said someone. 'No one here has seen much evidence that Jacob's pigs were here. We should not allow our prejudices against the man and our desire to have him feed us, move us to hang on his neck a rope that is not for him. Bakam who said it was Jacob's pigs that desecrated Chuwajo's grave has refused to come to the cemetery with us because he knew he was lying. What have we seen here in the cemetery? There is little evidence to show Jacob's pigs were even here, less desecrating a grave. Instead, it is Bakam's gunpowder that is loaded in Chuwajo's hand as if it were cartridge. Now we know why Bakam has refused to come to the cemetery.'

'God forbid bad thing,' somebody swore. 'Has the famine become so severe that some of us have become cannibals?'

'The chief's decision is ridiculous,' said Jacob's brother at last. 'My brother will not comply with it. Why should the ant suffer to gather food only for the rat to feed on it?'

'Koyan, are you calling the chief a rat?' someone asked.

'I am not calling him a rat,' said Jacob's brother. 'All I am saying is people should respect themselves and stop behaving like rats. If anyone wants to eat Jacob's food, why not say so instead of giving the phoney excuse of ghosts preventing people from going out to look for food? Why not simply say, Jacob, since your pigs have done this, your punishment is feeding this village for two weeks? That to me is more honourable than this absurdity.'

'Koyan, I agree with you,' someone said.

'I also agree with Koyan,' said another person. 'But I also agree with the chief. Let Jacob feed the village for two weeks as punishment, not because there are ghosts terrorising people. Where is the food outside that people can even go and get?'

'The judgment of the people is that Jacob must feed the whole village for two weeks,' said Adubu. 'This judgment has nothing to do with the reason given by the chief.'

There was a loud din of approbation of what Adubu said. The few voices of dissent in the crowd were swallowed up by the uproarious voices of approval.

'If Jacob does not give us the food himself, we will come and take it ourselves,' said Adubu.

Again there was another din of approbation of what Adubu had said.

Jacob listened to all the people were saying without saying anything. When there were courts and police in the country, he would have taken the matter to them. But now both the police and the courts were moneylenders and pig merchants like him looking for opportunities to squeeze money out of anyone in distress seeking their assistance. If he reports to the police, before they give him the protection he needed, the people would have descended on his house and carted away all he had. The court was even worse. It would take him ten years to get judgment from the court and he would have to feed the judge and his court clerks for all these years. It was far cheaper to feed the village for two weeks than the judge and his court for ten years or even more. What was more, it was better to feed people he knew than a judge he did not know. Rather than feed the chimpanzee he did not know, why not the monkey he knew? Also going to the court meant reporting the chief and those who supported him to the judge. It was like suing the entire village. This would lead to bad blood. After the case he would still have to live with the same people. It was better to submit to this bizarre and opportunistic decision of the chief than go to court or to the police.

Chapter Eighteen

At home Bakam was full of misgivings. He could not remember when he last saw a snake slough even in the bush while hunting. For a snake slough to be lying near his house was very ominous. For a hunter, a snake slough was bad luck. In his hunting, he had never seen a snake slough and continued the hunting. Although nothing bad had ever happened to him after seeing a snake slough, he believed it was because he had always abandoned whatever he was doing each time he saw the hoodoo. Now he believed that nothing bad would happen to him because immediately he saw the slough, he went back into his house.

For a while thoughts of the snake slough slipped out of his mind and were replaced by thoughts of money he found on the road. After talking with the bricklayer on the road and moving on, he had seen the money lying on the ground in front of him. Immediately he suspected it must be the bricklayer's money. It must have fallen off his pocket without him knowing. If the money were that of some other person who moved on the road earlier on, the bricklayer would have seen or stumbled on it if he were a blind man. It must be the money Jacob gave him that made him so happy and desperately defensive of the moneylender. He picked the money and put it in his pocket. All that was on his mind then was that he would keep the money and let the bricklayer suffer to look for it. Later he would return it to him and chide him for his carelessness. It was after he had put the money in his pocket that he heard the grunting of the pigs in the tall elephant grass.

Now he was wondering whether he should return the money to the bricklayer. He had no food in his house. Maybe he should use the money to buy foodstuff. Jacob who he was sure gave the money to the bricklayer was a bad man and the bricklayer who was given the money was also a bad man since he was now defending someone everyone in the village considered evil. It is always for the good of society that an evil man be deprived of means that he might use to oppress others. By holding onto the money, he would be doing society a lot of good. Maybe Bosuu the god of the earth intended to punish the bricklayer by making him lose the money. Maybe he would offend the god of the earth if he returns the money to the bricklayer. Maybe Bosuu intended to reward him for his abhorrence of the desecration of the cemetery and that was why he took the property of a person who did not see anything wrong with the desecration of the cemetery and gave it to him. But was it right to withhold the money from the bricklayer knowing the bricklayer needed it more than him and would have to pay Jacob whether or not the money was lost? But was the money the bricklayer's? Maybe it was someone else's money. He knew the bricklayer would not have the honesty to say it was not his money if he takes it to him. But he knew he was not honest with himself. There was no doubt the money was the bricklayer's. If he had any doubt about this, all he needed do to clear the doubt was to go to the bricklayer and ask if he had lost money and how much it was. If he told him an amount less or more than what he found on the road, he would know it was not his money. But won't the bricklayer go into the village telling everyone about money he had found and have everyone calling on him claiming it was his money? No he would not go to the bricklayer to ask him about the money. He needed it as badly as the bricklayer.

He was still thinking about the money and what he would do with it when he heard the bricklayer's voice outside his house. The bricklayer was exchanging greetings with someone whose voice he did not know. He had no doubt it was the money that had brought the bricklayer to his house. If not the money, nothing would bring him to his house so early in the morning and after he upbraided him the previous day. Almost instantly he decided that if the bricklayer asks for the money, he would give it to him because then there would be no doubt it was his money. But must he even wait for the bricklayer to ask for the money now that he was in his house? Shouldn't he just hand over the money to him? That would be more honourable than waiting to be asked. No, he must wait for the bricklayer to ask. No he must not wait.

The bricklayer having searched everywhere for the money without finding it decided to go to Bakam to ask if he saw any money on the road the previous day. Bakam was the first person he met on the road after leaving Jacob's house. So if the money fell on the road it was likely to be him that would find it. But if Bkam found the money would he give it to him? Well, Bakam was arrogant, but he was an honest man. If he found the money he would most likely give it to him. But he had done bad to Bakam. How would he undo it? Well, the hunter did not know or even suspect his treachery against him. He might not even be aware yet that evidence and circumstances now exist linking him to the desecration of Chuwajo's grave. But for his worry that he had wronged Bakam which made him to keep debating whether to ask the hunter if he found his money, he would have been to Bakam's house much earlier in the morning. When he finally decided to ask the hunter about the money, he went to his house on the double. He was sure Bakam on seeing the snake slough would not go to the cemetery but would stay at home. He was right. After exchanging greetings with someone passing by Bakam's house, he entered the house.

'It is the money isn't it?' Bakam asked the bricklayer after they had exchanged greetings.

The bricklayer's heart leapt with excitement and his face lit up with smiles. 'Yes,' he said, feverishly. 'Did you find it?'

'Yes, I did,' said Bakam. 'First, I wondered if it was your money or not and when I convinced myself it was your money, I wondered if I should give it to you or hold it seeing how you were supporting an evil man. But now that you have come to my house for it, I have no reason not to give it to you.' He brought out the money the way he picked it on the road and gave it to the bricklayer. 'Try to be a little more careful in holding money,' he said. 'It's not everyone who finds it that returns it.'

The bricklayer was so touched by Bakam's honesty that there was a loud crack in his voice when he spoke. 'Thank you very much,' he said, collecting the money. 'I will never forget this for as long as I live. Honest people like you are fading out everyday so much that someone has said honesty is now as scarce as ice water in hell.'

Bakam laughed. 'I would not put it so severely,' he said. 'Perhaps it is as scarce as water in the desert.'

'Yet you don't go to church,' said the bricklayer. 'I cannot understand you.'

'I was born the way you find me,' said Bakam 'I don't need the church to be who I am. All I need is my conscience. Good day.'

The bricklayer left Bakam's house happy he had found his money but sad that out of anger he had implicated in a heinous crime the man who found and returned his lost money to him. He might not forget Bakam's act of honesty and kindness for as long as he lived, but would he be able to live with himself knowing the grievous wrong he had committed against Bakam? It was too late to undo what he had done. Even if he were to remove the snake slough in front of Bakam's house, Bakam might not know and so would still not venture out of his house. If he knew, he might suspect him as the person who placed the slough in front of his house in the first place. It would be clear to him it was after he had come and gone that the hoodoo disappeared from the frontage of the house. Neither could he go to the cemetery now and remove the ash from Chuwajo's hand. The cemetery as far as he knew was now swarming with people. The best thing was for him to confess before the Father on Sunday. With a veil between him and the Father, the Father would not even know who was confessing. But this would not do. The only confession that would do was confession to the people of what he had done against Bakam. 'No, I cannot do that. How can I?' he cried. 'What would the Reverend Father think of me? What would other members of the church think of me? But I have done a great wrong to Bakam. Oh I am not better than Jacob's pigs.' Well, what can I do now? This is terrible,' he murmured as if afraid the bush would hear him. There was nothing he could do. What has happened has happened.

Chapter Nineteen

After his brother had told him what happened while he was away looking for his pigs, for a while Jacob sat wondering what to do. He was so shocked he could not think well. As it was said in Tounga, when the tortoise falls on its back, it would be so confused that it cannot even think. Jacob was a tortoise that had fallen on his back and was confused for a while. Even without anyone telling him, he knew his pigs had done a very outrageous thing. All those who were envious of his wealth would now rise up against him determined to pull him down. From what his brother told him, the earth priest and the people were not likely to go to the cemetery that night. He had to do something that night to remove the rope his pigs had hung around his neck. The rope he failed to hang on the pigs, they had hung on him. How was he to wriggle his head out of it? By now the whole village had heard what his pigs did to Chuwajo's grave. Even if he goes and erase the footprints of the pigs and other evidences of their visit to the cemetery, this would not change anything. But it was only Bakam who said he saw the footprints of the pigs at the cemetery. If he could go and erase the footprints and smoothen the burrowed soil of the cemetery, it would be Bakam's words against his tomorrow. Even Bakam did not say he saw the pigs desecrating Chuwajo's grave. All he said he saw were their footprints at the cemetery. If he could efface the footprints this night, Bakam would have a lot of proving to do tomorrow.

What was he to do? Like most people he was afraid of going to the cemetery at night for fear of the ghosts of the dead and other evil spirits that congregate there at night. It was because of that fear he had hastily walked past the cemetery when he was returning from searching for the pigs. That was before he learned of the desecration of Chuwajo's grave by his pigs. With his knowledge that a grave had been desecrated in the cemetery and by his pigs, his fear increased. Who would he get to go to the cemetery this night to efface the visit by the pigs? Perhaps the bricklayer would do it for him. But how was he to get the bricklayer that night. The bricklayer was not even likely to be at home. He must have travelled to Lilong or Denkita for the treatment of his ulcer. Even if he were at home, he would not go out in a perilous night like this to look for him. Neither would he send anyone in his house to go and call him. It is when you need people that you don't find anyone around you, he thought bitterly. People only come to you when they need you and not when you need them. This being the nature of people, he should use anyone that needed something from him.

He was still thinking of what to do when Sa'are came to his house to ask that he be given five measures of millet on credit. Throughout the day he and his family had not eaten. He had drank water and gone to lie down, but the crying of his children from hunger would not let him sleep. Even without the wailing of his children, his own hunger would not allow him to sleep. So he had to leave his house and go to Jacob's house to beg that he be given millet or any other foodstuff on credit since he had no money to pay for any. He had heard about the desecration of Chuwajo's grave. It was the reason that delayed his going to Jacob's house to ask for the credit. He had thought it was not proper to go and seek favour from a man who had just suffered such a misfortune. But in the end he had to go when he could no longer stand the wailing of his children and his own hunger. But he would not raise the issue of the pigs with Jacob unless the moneylender on his own raised it. People can be funny. If he raises the issue of the pigs with Jacob in order to console him, the moneylender may think he is mocking him and he was likely to be resentful.

After Sa'are had made his request, Jacob for a while did not say anything.

'Have you heard what I said,' Sa'are asked after a long interval of silence.

'I heard you,' Jacob said and lapsed into another silence. To Sa'are it was the most torturous silence he had had to endure.

'The village has turned into a stomach,' Jacob said at last. 'Anyone you see will only ask you of food. When this famine is over, we may find that we have no more heads to think and behave like human beings.'

'Things cannot be worse than they are,' said Sa'are in a voice that trembled with hunger.

While Sa'are was still talking, the two men heard the howling of a hyena. Jacob's eyes narrowed and for a moment his forehead was turned into a little farm of ridges and furrows. It was an indication he was in deep thought. 'This answers it,' he whispered at last. 'This answers it.' The hyena was going to the cemetery. It must have gotten a whiff of the smell of Chuwajo's exhumed body. If it was not going to the cemetery, Sa'are who had come to beg food from him must find a way of drawing it there. Tomorrow it must be the footprints of hyenas that would be found in the cemetery and not those of his pigs.

Sa'are sat looking at him thoughtfully.

'You heard the hyena howling?' Jacob asked with an expression near one of cheerfulness on his face.

'Yes,' Sa'are replied wondering where the question was leading to.

'I think it is hungry.'

Sa'are did not say anything probably because he thought there was nothing to say; probably because he was too hungry to comment on what was of no moment to him.

'I believe the hyena like you is hungry.'

Again Sa'are did not say anything. Instead he merely cleared his throat.

'I believe it is howling from hunger,' Jacob said with what appeared to Sa'are to be an amused expression. 'At the rate things are going,' he continued, 'very soon we will hear the sky crying from hunger. I believe the locusts ate the clouds in the sky before they came to earth.'

'My family is hungry,' Sa'are said, running out of patience. 'Since morning they have eaten nothing.'

'The hyena is also hungry,' said Jacob. 'I believe it too has eaten nothing since morning. I think you should take something first to the hyena before you take it to your family.'

Sa'are nearly screamed at him, but quickly checked himself. His family was at home waiting for him to bring food to them and only Jacob could give him the food. Anger would only destroy him and his family. He had to wait on the trifles of Jacob however irritating while his fundamental problems deteriorate beyond recovery. So instead of screaming at Jacob, only a faint frown appeared on his face.

'Everyone you see in this life carries a head and a headache,' said Jacob. 'You have your headache; I have mine. Your headache is what to eat; mine is how to ensure the envy of others does not consume me. My headache is how to ensure I am not brought down to the level of thinking of what to eat. No doubt you must have heard what Bakam said my pigs had done to Chuwajo's grave?'

'Yes.'

Yet he would not condole me. All people want from me is my wealth Jacob thought sourly. 'Go and lure the hyena howling out there to Chuwajo's grave,' he said with contempt in his heart. 'I want the footsteps of the hyena to replace those of my pigs in that cemetery. Let the desecration of the grave be by the hyenas and not by my pigs. You can go home and carry your bow and arrow, in case.'

'Life,' Sa'are sighed. 'It is so mean and miserable. What of the millet I requested for?' he asked.

'This thing won't take long,' said Jacob. 'As soon as you do what I ask, come back here. It is not even millet I will give you, but rice and palm oil as well. And you will not have to pay for them. They are free.'

Sa'are's face brightened. Fear is a terrible thing he thought. It makes it impossible for a man to think properly. But for fear, no one needed to tell Jacob that it was the smell of Chuwajoh's decomposing body that had brought out the hyena and that was where it was headed if it was not already there. Well, this was his opportunity. He would exploit Jacob's fear and squeeze out what he could.

Everyone knew that all that was needed to set a trap for a hyena and catch it was to place a big piece of meat on the trap and so he would start from that angle. 'What I need to lure the hyena to the grave is meat and I don't have it,' Sa'are said. 'But I know you will have it. Give me any meat you have and I will lure the hyena to the cemetery and to Chuwajo's grave.'

'In that case the smell of Chuwajo's decomposing body should lure them,' Jacob said.

Sa'are's heart sank. So he can still think with the fear I see on his face, he thought. Jacob would be trickier to handle than he had thought. 'The odour of a decomposing human body is the same with the odour of fermented locust beans,' he said, managing to maintain a straight face and a stable voice. 'You know hyenas have a strong aversion for fermented locust beans and so instead of being lured to the cemetery, the smell of Chuwajo's body would most certainly repel the hyena from the cemetery.'

Jacob did not know whether hyenas had an aversion for fermented locust beans or not and so could not refute what Sa'are had said. The question he would have asked that Sa'are would have had no answer for did not occur to him until Sa'are had left.

Without saying anything again, Jacob entered his room and brought three big chunks of fried meat and gave Sa'are. Sa'are almost seized the meat from him and literally fled the house. It was after he had left that it occurred to Jacob that the smell of Chuwajo's decomposing body would be far stronger than the smell of the meat he had given Sa'are to use to lure the hyena to the cemetery. If as Sa'are had said, hyenas were averse to the smell of fermented locust beans which he knew was similar to that of a decomposing human body, it would be useless trying to lure the hyena to the cemetery using his meat since the smell of the decomposing body would overwhelm the smell of his meat. If on the other hand what Sa'are had said about the aversion of hyenas to the smell of fermented locust beans was not true, using his meat was also unnecessary since the strong smell of the decomposing body would be enough to draw the hyena to the cemetery. He was sure Sa'are knew all these. He must be laughing at him now. He felt bad. As he sat feeling sad over how Sa'are had tricked him, he heard the howling of more hyenas. This told him like nothing else could that it was Chuwajo's decomposing body that had drawn the hyenas out of their caves for a feast. Sa'are was lying about a decaying human corpse repulsing hyenas. How could it even be when hyenas are pigs that nothing repels. 'The bastard!' he swore. Well, he would still come for the rice and palm oil. When he comes, he would receive the shock of his life. But he might not return. He might take the meat home and eat with his starving family. But meat is not food that satisfies anyone. He had to come back.

Sa'are hastened home with the meat, and as Jacob had thought, laughing. Today he had gotten Jacob in a way he believed no one ever thought possible. 'It is good to be smart,' he kept telling himself. None of the meat was going to the cemetery. He would give it to his family to eat before he receives the rice from Jacob. Jacob must be very scared to be parting with things like this. Before he got home, he had almost finished eating one chunk of meat. He gave the remaining two and what remained of the one he had eaten to his wife and children. After drinking water, he carried his hoe, bow and quiver that had only two arrows in it and headed for the cemetery. Even at a much younger age, he had no fear of the dead, and so had no fear going to the cemetery. He had a clear mind of what to do at the cemetery when he gets there. Jacob might be stupid because of his fear, but he had to do something to earn the meat he had given him and the rice and palm oil he promised him. If Jacob discovered he had only conned him and did nothing to earn what he had given him, he might do what he would regret. He knew Jacob to be a very mean person.

'Where are you going?' his wife asked him.

'You and the children were crying when I came in; what were you crying for?' he asked the wife, a little friendlier now that he had eaten the meat.

'Food,' said the wife,' more pleasant now that she was eating the meat.

'You heard the hyena howling not long ago?' Sa'are asked not in a haste to leave.

'Yes,' said the wife.

'What did you imagine it was howling for?'

'Food,' replied the wife, almost amiably.

'Fine,' said Sa'are 'Apart from the meat in your mouths now, there is no food in this house. I am going out there to hunt for food with the hyena. With any luck the hyena might provide us with the food we need so badly.'

'What of the hoe?'

'I am going there to farm with it.'

Chapter Twenty

Bakam was still at home when he heard the angry voices of people moving closer to his house. At first he thought it was Jacob they were cursing and swearing at, but he soon heard someone in the angry crowd saying he did not know he was such an evil and treacherous person. His heart kicked violently against his ribs. What had he done to deserve this vicious attack? Well, whatever it was, he would soon know since the crowd was moving towards his house. Soon the crowd was in front of the house.

'Bakam come out and tell us why you desecrated Chuwajo's grave only to lie against Jacob's pigs!' someone in the crowd hollered.

With his heart beating fast, Bakam came out to meet the crowd that was behaving like a drunken horse without reins in its mouth. The earth priest appeared the only sober man in the mob. 'What is the matter?' he asked

'As if he does not know,' someone hissed.

'What are we waiting for?' somebody shouted. 'Burn his house.'

'Not yet,' said the earth priest. 'Bakam, why did you refuse to come with us to the cemetery today?'

Bakam was silent. The people did not know what he knew about snake sloughs. So if he tells them he was prevented from going to the cemetery by a snake slough he saw in front of his house, they would not understand.

The people took his silence as confirmation of what they suspected to be the reason of his refusal to be at the cemetery.

'Bakam, why did you desecrate Chuwajo's grave only to turn round to accuse Jacob's pigs?' asked Adubu.

'What!' Bakam cried. 'This cannot be true. If I desecrated his grave, I wouldn't have been so stupid to carry the news of the desecration to the village.' He was now sweating profusely.

'That you told the village of the desecration does not mean much. The tortoise is known for his tricks of rushing to report to the lion crimes he has committed,' someone said.

'There is no doubt you were the one who carried the news to the village yesterday,' said Adubu. 'But why were you not at the cemetery today when it matters most? Right now I have only two thoughts in my mind. Either you desecrated Chuwajo's grave yesterday and tried to pin the blame on Jacob's pigs or the pigs did so and you thinking you had convinced everyone of the pigs' sacrilege returned to the cemetery at night to further desecrate the grave and indeed other graves.'

'Besides the fact that I was not at the cemetery, what makes you think I desecrated Chuwajo's grave?' Bakam asked, pulling himself together.

'We found very few pigs footprints,' said Adubu; 'but found a lot of gunpowder in one of Chuwajo's hands where a muscle had been cut apparently for charm making.'

'Treachery is about,' said Bakam. 'Someone must have gone to the cemetery at night to free Jacob and implicate me.'

'Who could that be?' asked Jacob, angrily. 'Did that person stop you from coming to the cemetery this morning?'

'He could be right Jacob,' said the earth priest. 'But like you said, his refusal to go to the cemetery makes his story difficult to believe.'

'I have a good reason not to be at the cemetery,' said Bakam. Since they were now hinging his guilt on his absence at the cemetery, he has to tell them why he was not there. 'When I came out of my house this morning to go to the cemetery, I saw that snake slough lying there,' he said, pointing at the snake slough still lying on the ground not far away from the crowd. I thought if I walk past the snake slough something bad would happen to me. That was why I did not go to the cemetery.'

Most people reeled with laughter. It was either Bakam had gone mad or he was admitting his guilt in a ridiculous way. The latter seemed more probable. But the earth priest did not laugh. He knew hunters were people with many beliefs and this could be one of them.

'You have not walked past the snake slough, yet something terrible has happened to you,' said Gochap.

'Perhaps something worse would have happened to him,' someone said.

'Are you then to remain in your house till the snake slough develops wings and fly away?' asked Gochap.

'It is only for today. Tomorrow I am free to leave my house,' said Bakam.

'This is very funny,' said Watto

'No, I think it is stupid,' said Adubu

'Not so stupid,' somebody said. 'All of us here are under the bondage of one superstitious belief or the other. Why should we hold Bakam to ridicule because his own belief has failed him?'

'What Bakam has said now shows it was a hunter that cut the muscle from the dead man's hand to make charm,' said Jacob's brother. 'The hunter and superstition hunt together in the bush.'

'Jacob, did you go to the cemetery last night to rope Bakam in?' asked the earth priest.

Jacob's heart sank. 'I didn't and couldn't do such a thing,' he said avoiding the earth priest's eye.

'I was just wondering,' said the earth priest.

For a moment no one spoke.

'Jacob may deny going to the cemetery to wipe out evidence of his pigs sacrilege and some of us may believe him, but what of Chuwajo's flesh and blood on the snouts of his pigs that we paraded them through the village with yesterday? What of the red earth in their hooves?' Bakam asked breaking the silence. 'It is not difficult to find out if a man is suffering from elephantiasis of the scrotum. Just lift up his clothes.'

Now that he was in trouble Garu his friend had not spoken one word in his defence. Instead he appeared to be hiding from him by standing behind a fat man that completely screened him from his view. When a corpse begins to decompose and gives foul odour, friends desert it, he thought, dejectedly.

'Which flesh and blood?' Jacob's brother asked, angrily. 'Were those dark smears what you call human blood? How do we know it was Chuwajo's flesh that was on the snouts of the pigs and not that of a decaying animal? You could have smeared the pigs with the blood and flesh of any decomposing animal.'

'I was not the one that drove them home. It was Watto and he is here to say which blood and flesh he believed the pigs had on their snouts,' said Bakam.

'Watto, what have you to say to that?' asked Adubu.

'I don't want to say anything to that,' said Watto. 'All I know is that Jacob's pigs ate my cocoyam.'

'Who is the vulture that desecrated Chuwajo's grave and the other graves in the cemetery?' someone wondered aloud, rhetorically.

'When the man on top of a palm tree fouls the air, the flies are confused,' said Adubu. 'In their confusion, they will wonder where the foul air is coming from and they will start flying in different directions.'

'That maybe true,' said Gochap. 'But a goat never passes its excrement in lumps. It passes its excrement in little seeds. Bakam could not have done this. It is not in his nature.'

'After the rat has messed up the place, it might escape leaving the sluggish snail which happened by to take the blame,' someone said.

'If mushrooms are tampered with, the tortoise is the prime suspect because that is its food,' said another person.

'If the owl cried at night and in the morning the child died, who killed it?' somebody asked.

'The witch of course!' cried many voices.

'Owls are witches!' cried a lone voice.

'So are pigs,' said another person.

'I believe it was Jacob's pigs that did the most horrible things we saw at the cemetery,' said the old man that Jacob insulted the previous day. 'Remember Jacob I told you it will not be well with you; now look at it. I did not even know my curse would find fulfilment so soon.'

'Old man, don't celebrate yet,' said another man. 'Doubt like a little child holding the hand of a blind old man seems to be holding the hand of each suspect and walking him away from the crime leaving the cemetery at the mercy of an unknown vulture,' said Gochap. Other people began to ventilate their minds and their feelings.

'Doubt seems to be shielding every crook.'

'The days are indeed evil.'

'This famine walks on four legs and carries four heads.'

'The famine is holding a sword against everyone's throat.'

'It is now two days since I last ate any food and the last time I ate was in my dream.'

'Who cleared his throat?'

'Maybe it is the famine.'

'Only the famine is belching while everyone is yawning.'

'That is not true. The vultures are belching too. So are the flies.'

'Jacob's pigs are belching too.'

'Who is the pig talking of Jacob's pigs?'

'People clear their throats now than they belch.'

'We ate the locusts together with the vultures.'

'But they are now eating our corpses alone.'

'If you could not fly with the locusts after they attacked our crops, you may yet fly in a vulture when you die.'

'If you can't fly in an aeroplane while alive, you may yet fly in a vulture when you die.'

'If you die now and cannot make the heaven of God in the sky, you will make that of the vultures in the sky.'

You either feed termites or vultures.'

'You are either eaten by vultures of the air or vultures of the earth.'

'Which vultures are vultures of the earth?'

'Termites.'

'We must find out which vulture desecrated our cemetery,' said the earth priest. 'I am not a seer. I am only the earth priest of Bosuu the god of the earth. He is my eyes. I will go and place before Bosuu the god of the earth the demand of the people for justice. In three days you shall all know what Bosuu decrees.'

Chapter Twenty-One

From Bakam's house, the bricklayer went straight to the mission hospital at Lilong for his ulcer to be treated. For the first time the doctor attending to him told him he was suffering from peptic ulcer. The doctor also told him that hunger and extreme distress are some of the causes of his type of ulcer. Immediately he knew Jacob had caused his sickness.

For close to a year, he had gone to Jacob begging he be paid his money to no avail. Jacob always had one excuse or the other not to pay him. At a point, it even looked like the moneylender was avoiding him. There were times when out of worry, he would lie down and tears would be dropping from his eyes in tiny bits. Because Jacob did not pay him, he had no money to buy grains to feed his family after the attack of the locusts. Knowing all these, when the doctor told him the causes of ulcer, he knew what caused his own. Jacob had almost killed him.

'Jacob, it will never be well with you,' he swore, panting with hate. God will surely judge him. As for him, there was nothing he could do. Jacob was too powerful for him to challenge. He would crush him like a bedbug. He did not want to die. Though there was little to live for, life was still better than death and he would cling to it to the last day of his allotted days.

'It is so awful to know I went the length I went to desecrate Chuwajo's grave to save a man who had so ill-treated me,' he mourned. 'But it is more awful to know I have implicated an innocent man who had the honesty to give me my lost money. How do I undo this great evil I have so treacherously contrived?'

On his way back home, he was full of painful thoughts. Jacob who had given him ulcer, he had risked his life to exonerate from a crime his pigs committed. Bakam who had found and gave him the money to treat his ulcer, he had implicated in a monstrous crime. Was there ever an ugly and tragic irony like this? At a point he had so much self-contempt that he walked to a nearby gorge to jump into the yawning crevice. But as he got nearer to the gorge, his resolve began to weaken. 'It is a sin to take one's life,' he murmured to himself. 'If I do such a sinful thing I should be sure of my place in hell. Besides, who will take care of my children?' He began walking back to the road.

'I will never want to set my eyes on Jacob again,' he said to himself after he had regained the road. 'That should be enough punishment for him. He likes people coming to his house and prostrating before him. He will never see me in his house again,' he swore, full of bile. 'Such a bad man! Bakam, please forgive me though I don't deserve your forgiveness. If only you would repent and accept Jesus Christ as your lord and saviour, there is no reason you will not make heaven. You are even more honest than the Reverend Father. The last harvest of the church, the Father could not account for it. Maybe it was eaten by locusts – the locusts in his heart.'

'Worry is like fart, unless you release it through the lower mouth, it would swell up your stomach and the next thing is that you are purging,' said a man behind the bricklayer.

The bricklayer spun round to see it was Bonga from his village that had caught up with him while he was tormented by his worries. How long had Bonga being walking behind him? How much of what he had been saying to himself had Bonga heard? His heart was beating very fast. If Bonga heard all he had said, he was finished.

'Bonga, you scared me,' he said in a poor attempt to explain his fear. 'Why did you come sneaking behind me like a ghost?'

'I am Chuwajo's ghost,' Bonga said and laughed.

The bricklayer could not believe his ears. Surely Bonga couldn't have said he was Chuwajo's ghost.

'This is not a laughing matter?' the bricklayer said rather too severely. 'You don't tiptoe behind people like the tortoise or the devil.'

'You don't have anything to worry about,' said Bonga. 'Even if I had been walking behind you all the way from Lilong, I could not have heard anything of the things you were mumbling to yourself.'

The bricklayer was relieved. But he had to be more careful. You don't talk to yourself on grave matters like this without looking over your shoulders now and then. It is not for nothing a gossip would first look at the approach before he begins his gossip. 'No one can survive two famines like this in a life time,' he said in a light-hearted voice.

'If you listen well, you will hear the trees yawning of hunger,' said Bonga.

'It is so frightful,' said the bricklayer.

'It is not the famine that is so frightful,' said Bonga. 'It is the fact that people have lost their consciences.'

What does he mean by *people have lost their consciences*? What does he know? the bricklayer wondered, fearfully.

'At this time when we should have pity for each other, people keep hiking the prices of their foodstuff as if they had been told God has died.'

'That might be the thoughts of people. But God is still alive,' the bricklayer said, glibly.

'God, my brother lives only on the lips of men,' said Bonga. 'It cost nothing for him to live on the lips. But in the heart, you pay a lot. That is why when you go to the hearts of most men it is the devil you find.'

Would he be able to walk with this man all the way to Tounga? the bricklayer wondered, despairingly. He did not say anything.

'God is like an advice,' the bricklayer heard Bonga saying. 'It cost you nothing to give someone God, but it cost you a lot to receive him from another person.'

'When did you leave home today?' the bricklayer asked changing the topic.

'Sometime towards noon.'

'What is happening about Chuwajo's desecrated grave?'

'It is not only Chuwajo's grave that has been desecrated; many other graves have also been desecrated.'

This was news to the bricklayer. When he spoke, his voice carried his shock.

'This is terrible. Who desecrated the other graves?'

'They said it is Bakam and the hyenas.'

They said it is Bakam he repeated what Bonga had said in his mind. So the people jumped to the conclusion he wanted them to. Before Bakam returned his lost money, this news would have made him happy. Now it made him sad. 'Hyenas, this is terrible!' he muttered after an interval of silence.

'Hyenas, my brother.'

'Since when have hyenas started going to cemeteries to devour the dead?' asked the bricklayer, rhetorically. 'This is terrible!'

'Yes, it is. But I think what is more terrible is the involvement of human beings in the defilement of the cemetery. We are giving the devil too much space in our lives.'

'You said Bakam is being suspected of involvement in the desecration of the cemetery?' asked the bricklayer, struggling to keep his voice stable. 'Why is he suspected?'

'The central muscle in Chuwajo's hand near the wrist was found severed with a knife and what looked like gunpowder loaded where the muscle was severed. Bakam being the only hunter with a gun and gunpowder is suspected of severing the dead man's muscle to make charm. To make matters worse, Bakam was not at the cemetery when people went to see what he was screaming over the previous day.'

The whole thing worked the way he hoped it would the bricklayer thought, despairingly. 'Chuwajo's muscle was severed and gunpowder was loaded in his mutilated hand? This is bad,' he said in a shocked voice. 'But why should Bakam do such a thing?'

'I wonder, my brother,' said Bonga, meditatively. 'Bakam is such an honest and good man that I do not think he could have done such a thing. But the problem is why did Bakam not go to the cemetery with other people?'

'Yes; you said Bakam did not go to the cemetery. Given his outrage the previous day, his absence at the cemetery must excite curiosity and suspicion, especially when a sacrilege such as the one you told me is found committed at the cemetery,' said the bricklayer. He had warned himself not to support Bonga too strongly in his belief that Bakam was innocent.

'He was unfortunately not at the cemetery. That is what made most people believe he was the one who desecrated the cemetery only to accuse the pigs.'

'One can hardly blame them.'

'But you too were not at the cemetery.'

'I have a good reason for not being at the cemetery,' the bricklayer said in a tight voice. 'I went to Lilong for medication. As you can see that is where I am returning from.'

'Bakam also had a reason for not going to the cemetery. Only that his reason is not a good one like yours. A snake slough lying in front of his house prevented him from going to the cemetery.'

The whole thing had worked out the way he planned, the bricklayer thought, sorrowfully. 'A snake slough? But that is ridiculous, isn't it?' he said in a husky voice. 'A reason like that can only make people suspect him more than they would have if he had no reason at all.'

'Yes, it may sound ridiculous; but you know hunters are people full of superstition.'

'In that case, they are more liable to believe in charms than anyone else.'

Bonga was shocked to hear the bricklayer saying something similar to what Jacob's brother said in Bakam's house. Reason is everywhere. Whoever you see carries his reason with him in his hair and fingernails. It is what sustains his life. Those who say the bricklayer is mad need their own heads examined.

'For me I don't believe Bakam did what he is accused of,' Bonga said. 'I think some evil person set him up. Bakam is too honourable for such despicable act.'

The bricklayer's heart quaked. Bonga was getting closer and closer to the truth. 'Well, you may have your reasons,' he said cautiously, 'but given the noise Bakam made yesterday over the desecration of Chuwajo's grave, it is difficult to accept that a mere snake slough prevented him from going to the cemetery with the people when it mattered most.'

'That is true,' said Bonga. 'But if he is innocent as I think he is, he would not know refusing to go to the cemetery because of the snake slough would have grave implications for him.'

'You are right,' the bricklayer said, wishing the journey would soon be over for him to be free of this torture.

'You see if I were Bakam and I had his superstition about snake sloughs, on seeing a snake slough in front of my house, I would not have jumped to the conclusion it was left their by a snake. I would have wondered if someone planted it there.'

The bricklayer was so paralysed with fear he could not even think, lest say anything. His only luck was that he was walking in front of Bonga. If they were facing each other, the guilt on his face would not require him to tell Bonga with his mouth he was the one who set Bakam up. Even with the luck of walking in front of Bonga, he was not sure his back was not telling the man something.

'If Bakam was set up as I think he was,' he heard Bonga saying, 'the person who set him up, if he knew of the superstition of hunters concerning snake sloughs, might have placed the snake slough in front of his house to prevent him from going to the cemetery.'

Short of calling his name as the person who had set Bakam up, Bonga had arrived at the whole truth without knowing it.

'But who do you think would have set Bakam up?' he heard himself asking Bonga. Later he was to wonder where he got the brainwave and courage to ask this question that gave him respite from Bonga's torturous permutations.

It seemed Bonga did not expect this question and so for a while he could not respond to it. 'That's the problem,' he said after a long interval of silence. 'It must be someone that bears him a grudge. You see in this life you can never tell who hates you and who likes you. We all flash our teeth at each other in hypocrisy, leaving our real feelings in our hearts.'

'Could it be Jacob? At least we all know he would bear Bakam a grudge for making so much noise about the desecration of Chuwajo's grave by his pigs.'

'It could be, though I have always found out that people I suspect of doing one thing or the other are not the ones. Suspicion can be so misleading.'

'It is shocking to hear that hyenas also invaded the cemetery,' the bricklayer said in a voice that sounded casual, but with an intention to switch the conversation from Bakam to the hyenas. Hopefully by the time they were through with any conversation on the hyenas, they would have reached the village and parted ways.

'Yes, hyenas,' Bonga said. 'From what I saw in the cemetery, we all have to close and lock our doors well these days when we go to sleep. If the hyenas could do what they did at the cemetery, they would soon enter the village.'

'It is terrible,' said the bricklayer, more relaxed now that the conversation has shifted to the hyenas.

'It is indeed,' said Bonga. 'The frightening thing is that hyenas in the village have joined the hyenas of the jungle to prey on us. Against the hyenas in the village, there is no remedy.'

The bricklayer could not say anything.

'The devil surely has people who are doing his bidding in the village,' Bonga said. 'Why should a man be this heartless to his fellow man, his fellow man that is dead?'

'When I heard the howling of those hyenas the previous night, I had a creeping sensation in my head that evil is abroad. It is so horrifying to know they descended on the cemetery like the locusts they are,' said the bricklayer.

'The hyenas seem to be learning bad things from us,' Bonga said.

Won't he leave desecration of the cemetery by people alone for a moment? the bricklayer wondered despairingly. He did not say anything.

'Do you know something?' the bricklayer heard Bonga asking him.

'No,' he said, wondering what was coming next.

'Like me, the earth priest does not seem to think Bakam could have desecrated Chuwajo's grave.'

The bricklayer was not unduly surprised by this. He had always thought that with his sharp mind which was as uncanny and awesome as his one eye, the earth priest was capable of seeing through anything. 'What did he do or say that gave you this impression?' he asked Bonga.

'He specifically asked Jacob, whether he went to the cemetery in the night to wipe out evidence of his pigs desecration of the cemetery and implicate Bakam.'

The bricklayer was so startled he heaved a sigh that luckily for him was not heard by Bonga because he was talking again.

'For the earth priest to ask such a question, I believe there was much more that he knew, but did not let on,' Bonga said. 'You know how deep the man is.'

Well, it is Jacob's funeral, the bricklayer thought. He deserves whatever is coming to him. 'If the earth priest said this, then Jacob is in trouble,' he said.

'He said so,' said Bonga; 'and as you said, Jacob is in trouble. But this might be small trouble compared to the trouble the chief asked Jacob to carry for two weeks without giving him even a pad to carry it on.'

'What trouble did the chief ask Jacob to carry?'

'He said for the next two weeks Jacob is to feed the entire village.'

This was shocking to the bricklayer and for a while, he did not say anything. 'But this is a strange punishment. Why did the chief pass such a judgment on Jacob?' he asked at last.

'He said for the next two weeks the ghosts of the dead men whose graves had been desecrated would haunt the village so much that no one can go out to find food. So for the two weeks people will remain at home, Jacob will have to feed them.'

'This is funny.'

'Indeed. But it is funny in a wonderful way. At least for the next two weeks, I don't have to worry about what to eat.'

'That is if Jacob complies with the absurdity.'

'He has no choice. It is no longer the chief's judgment but the people's judgment and he knows it.'

'This is wonderful!' exclaimed the bricklayer, excitedly. 'Jacob's chickens have come home to roost.'

'Do you know what the earth priest said when we were leaving Bakam's house?' Bonga asked.

The bricklayer held his breath. 'No, I don't.'

'He said he would consult his god to reveal the real culprits that desecrated the cemetery. So very soon the wind would blow and the anus of the fowl would be exposed.'

By now the two men had reached Tounga and the bricklayer was relieved to be rid of Bonga as he bade him farewell and walked towards his house.

Chapter Twenty-Two

What most people did not know was that Jacob was a coward and a vain man at heart. He had mortal fear for confrontation of any kind and there was nothing he cherished like people genuflecting before him asking for one favour or the other or bowing to greet him in recognition of his greatness. Inside him was always a longing to be hailed by others. Where that failed, he felt empty and unhappy. When people came before him grovelling because they were looking for a loan or some other favour, they gave him courage and confidence he did not have and invest in him a simmering pride that knew no moderation in its exultation. Now with most people speaking insultingly against him, he was trembling like a leaf within if he was only swaying like a branch without. The earth priest had spoken with his one eye looking like an unforgiving oracle. His one eye seemed to hold all knowledge of the earth including what had happened, but had for reasons known only to him decided not to reveal what it knew.

Like anyone, he was shocked that a muscle was removed from Chuwajo's hand and gunpowder was poured where the muscle was removed. Like Gochap said, whoever did this the locusts must have left with his heart. It was so horrible and heartless. Who could have done such a thing? Though Bakam was being accused, he did not think Bakam would do such a thing. Bakam might be his worst enemy now, he would not say the owl killed the chicken just because he did not like the owl. Could Sa'are have done it? Was it why he was not at the cemetery with other people? But he did not ask him to do such a thing. Well, there was something good for him in what was done. If Sa'are committed the sacrilege, it meant he could not turn round to blackmail him.

Three days after the chief and the people passed their judgment, he was at home restless. He lay back on his reclining chair his hands either folded on his chest or on his forehead. This was the worst problem he had ever encountered in his life. He had heard people saying it is a man's property that involves him in disputes. It was now he understood the full meaning of that saying. This was more than a dispute. It looked like a fire that would consume him or a flood that would drown him. His pigs had invited home a monster that would swallow him and them. People had spoken against him with a rudeness he never thought possible. He the wealthiest man in the village was being affronted even by people indebted to him. It was unbelievable.

But the real terror was the chief's sentence; no the people's sentence. The only motive of the sentence was to impoverish him by making him feed the village. In his life, he had never seen a ghost though he had heard people saying they had seen the ghost of their dead relation or some other dead person. Five years ago a woman died in the village. A year later, her husband travelled to Moruwa a far away town and returned with the frightful tale of seeing his dead wife selling tomatoes in Moruwa. There was also the tale of Boto who died many years ago. Before his death, he was working in Kanza and erecting a building in Menka. He died before completing the building. One day his acquaintance who did not know of his demise met him in a restaurant and he begged the acquaintance to take some money to his mother at Menka for the completion of the building. The acquaintance who was travelling through Menka and who knew Boto's mother accepted to deliver the message only to arrive Menka and be shown Boto's old grave. He fainted out of shock and had to be taken to hospital. He had heard all these tales. So stories about ghosts were not strange to him. But what he found strange and ridiculous in the chief's ghosts tale and judgment was that the ghosts of Chuwajo and other dead people whose graves were desecrated would be haunting the people of Tounga and so they should remain at home. If Chuwajo's or anyone's ghost would haunt anyone, it should be him or his pigs and whoever else desecrated the cemetery. The rest of the people were innocent. And if the ghosts were to haunt people, how would remaining at home secure them from the haunting ghosts?

Well, both he and the people knew he was complying with the judgment not because of the chief's phoney reason, but because of his fear that the people might invade his house and take all he had if he did not feed them. The chief himself knew he was not very much regarded by the people and his absurd judgment would have only recommended him for derision if it were not that it benefited the people.

His brother had told him to ignore the threat of the people and feed no one, but he had rejected his brother's advice as the voice of madness. If the mad voice of his brother collides with the mad voice of the people, he knew where victory lay. So he was feeding the people to avoid that collision.

But just two days of feeding the village had nearly finished one barn of millet. Each person seemed to have developed two stomachs to eat his food. As soon as people finished eating, they were hungry again. It was like there were locusts in their stomachs that ate what they had eaten and flew away. If he would have to feed the people at this rate, by the time the two weeks were over, he would have nothing to eat like everyone else. When he submitted to the chief's judgment he knew it was going to eat deep into his barns, but did not know it was going to eat so deep in only two days. Clearly, all the grains in his barns and his cocoyam and yam would be gone by the time the two weeks expire. He might even have to sell his pigs to buy grains to feed the village before the end of the two weeks. He would have to take the matter to the court at Lilong. But he would have to live with the people of the village after the court case. Well, he had to live with himself first before living with anyone. He was not sure he would live with himself after feeding the village for two weeks. He must go to court. The court certainly would make an order nullifying the absurd judgment of the chief. But would it? 'The court in this country is like a fly,' he murmured. 'When it lands on your wound, it opens it up. Like a monkey, you cannot trust the court with bananas. If you have a boil on your head and ask the monkey to carry your banana home, it would gobble it up on the way. Trying to get justice from the court is like trying to draw water from a well with a sieve. There is no point asking a blind man to find a needle for you or a cripple to fetch water for you from the river.'

As he sat outside his house thinking fearfully of his condition, a man walked past without greeting him. He knew the man and the man knew him, yet he walked past him without greeting him. It was not that the man did not see him. He knew he saw him because the man had looked in his direction before looking away. The convention is that the person who moves past another sitting or meets him at a place should first greet the person he meets or the person he is walking past. He had always wondered why this should be so. As a child, he thought it ought to be the other way round. The person who has walked to another person's house should be tired and ought to be greeted first by the person sitting in the house. But society thinks differently. Greetings must first come from the person on his feet to the person sitting. He saw this as another instance of giving more to a person who has. So the man on the road was the one to first greet him. But he only looked at him and walked on.

It was very painful. It was the first time someone would walk past him at such close range without greeting him. He was feeding the people now and they were treating him in this shabby manner; what would happen if he finished feeding them and had no more wealth?

After sitting for a while outside, he decided it was better he sits inside his house than outside where he would receive this kind of humiliating treatment. He was about going into his house when the Catechist of his church came by.

The Catechist was a loudmouth with no bridle on his lips. He was a man with many faults. One of his faults was that he often spoke carelessly without regard to the feelings of others. He was also known by most people as a philanderer. Two years ago he impregnated a chorister of his church. The scandal nearly tore the church apart. Somehow the Catechist survived it without being removed as Catechist. As he seduced women for himself, it was rumoured he arranged them for the Reverend Father who was also said to suffer from *King David's infirmity*. The Reverend Father was known for his condemnation of drunkenness, but not for his censure of fornication. In all his preaching in the church, he had something to say against the sin that led to the mortal sin of incest in the cave, but not for the mortal sin itself. Perhaps because of his liaison with women, he seemed to nurse an unholy bias against men. In all his preaching, he reserved his harsh words for the menfolk. A woman in his eyes was hardly capable of sin on her own. It was the men who were drunks that cause the women to sin. If there was a quarrel between a man and his wife and they came to him for settlement, he reserved his counselling for the man alone, sometimes even to the embarrassment of the woman. In most of his preaching, the Reverend Father always told the story of three clergy men who met after a long separation and confided in each other their weaknesses as *men of God.* One said his major problem was money. He just could not keep his itchy fingers from pilfering some of the monies of the church. The other said his problem was drunkenness. Before he mounts the pulpit, he must have a glass of *the cause of Lot's shame.* The third said his own weakness was his tongue. He was incapable of holding his tongue and keeping any secret. To the shock of his fellow clergymen who had already made their confessions, he said the moment he was out of the room they were making their confessions he would spill the beans to anyone that cared to listen. Some church members said the Reverend Father was not telling the story as they knew it. They said there was no drunk among the three clergymen but a womanizer.

To return to the Catechist, most people wondered why a scandalous man like him should be made a Catechist only to cause many people to backslide in the faith. Some people said he was made Catechist because he was the pimp of the Reverend Father. After performing catechism for the parishioners, he performed a special kind of catechism for the Reverend Father in the inner sanctuaries of debauchery according to the consecrated scriptures of pimps.

Now walking past Jacob sitting in front of his house, the Catechist asked with a sneer on his face, 'how are your pigs Jacob?'

'They are as fine as the girls in the choir,' Jacob replied, seething with rage.

Jacob's reply should have warned the Catechist he was treading on dangerous ground, but he was a man with an inert sense of danger.

'What your pigs did is terrible,' he said, the sneer on his face expanding. 'Pigs are dirty creatures.'

How can this louse that comes to collect tithes from him have the nerves to say pigs are dirty creatures? Jacob wondered, angrily. Was it not from his sales of the pigs that he got money to give the church as tithes? How many times had the church returned his money to him because it was gotten from the sale of dirty pigs? It was so annoying. But he still managed to control his anger and said nothing.

'What your pigs did is terrible,' said the Catechist, oblivious of how Jacob felt.

'It is no more terrible than impregnating little girls,' Jacob said with a wild look on his face. If a man does not think twice before climbing a donkey, the donkey should not think twice before throwing him off.

What the Catechist said next showed he was a reckless man that would not think twice before climbing a donkey. 'Jacob, people are saying you are a vulture; are you one?'

Though Jacob knew the Catechist for his uncouth tongue, he was nevertheless shocked by the rudeness of his verbal attack. For a while he could not say anything. When at last he found his tongue, he spoke with the anger of a man who had been trifled with.

'You and the Father are worse vultures than me, feasting on our women and on the fears of the flock,' he charged at the Catechist, the veins of his neck rippling with anger.

Though the Catechist knew he had sorely provoked Jacob he was shocked and alarmed by the intensity of Jacob's anger. With his mouth agape, he hurriedly walked away, occasionally looking back to see if Jacob was following him with a machete.

Not long after the Catechist was gone, Jacob's brother came.

'Koyan, the locusts have returned and they are only in my farm,' said Jacob, a little relieved to see his brother.

'It is not the locusts that returned Jacob,' said his brother, looking quite distraught. 'It is the wind of opportunity that you followed to find wealth that has returned to take the wealth from you. As the honey bird leads honey hunters to honey, it sometimes leads them to a den of lions.'

Chapter Twenty-Three

On the eve of the day the people were to go to the earth priest to hear what he had heard from Bosuu the god of the earth, Jacob could not sleep. He kept turning on his bed, but never finding a comfortable side of his body which he could lie on and get some sleep. Each side of his body was aching him.

What would the earth priest say he had heard from Bosuu the god of the earth? he kept wondering. He had so much fear for Bosuu the god of the earth. The god of the earth was not a god he could defy and not suffer severe consequences. He knew of the line of fresh raffia in the shrine that no supplicant crossed. He knew how Gola who defecated in the river where the village fetched its drinking water was cursed by the god. Before an assembly of the village, the earth priest had said to Gola, 'since you committed this evil, Bosuu the god of the earth says your land would no longer grow crops for you to eat and defecate in our rivers. If anyone lends his land to you, the curse of Bosuu will follow you to that land and to the person who lent it to you. If you drink water, it will be like flames of fire in your stomach. Go.' From that year Gola's crops started failing. His wife left him and his children started dying one after the other. When he could no longer stand it, he went and drowned himself in the river he defecated in. Also Zokom who stole yam from Boma's farm became blind after Bosuu had placed a curse on him. He was on his farm when a grain of sand fell into his eye. Though it was in one eye the sand fell, Zokom went blind in both eyes. Both Zokom and Boma were Christians. Yet, they were ruined by the curse of the god. The very sight of the earth priest inspired fear and faith in his god. If the priest was so frightening, the god whose shadow was on the priest was more awesome and severe in upholding his own judgment.

If he disobeys any order the god of the earth makes against him, he was sure his pigs which burrow into the earth would all die and he might even die with them since like everyone else he walked upon the earth.

The sentence the chief passed on him had almost ruined him. If the earth priest comes up with an equally draconian judgment, he would have had his own. He tried to imagine what the earth priest would say the god of the earth had told him, but could not come up with anything that looked like what a god might tell his priest. But he knew that gods behave like their priests. The earth priest was a strange and severe man and the judgment of his god was likely to be strange and severe.

Early in the morning people started going to the earth priest's shrine in droves. It appeared the whole village was going to the shrine. Jacob and his brother were among the last people that went to the shrine. Jacob's brother being a devout Christian had told Jacob not to go, but he did not heed his brother's counsel. He saw going to the shrine that day as a summon by the earth priest. It was unthinkable not to answer that summon. Though he knew going to the shrine would give his enemies an opportunity to sneer at him, particularly when the earth priest would be handing down the verdict of his god on him, their sneers were nothing compared to the consequences of not answering the summon of the earth priest.

Like on the first day, the earth priest came out of the shrine to address the people. He was surprised by the number of people he saw. For a while he stood and surveyed the people with his one eye without saying anything. Most people flinched when his eye fell on them. Today his eye seemed to hold all the secrets and mysteries of the world. To Jacob, though the earth priest did not speak, his eye was telling him terrible things.

The earth priest began to speak by mumbling some inaudible words perhaps to his god; then began to speak audibly: 'No man leaves his eyes behind him. We all walk with our eyes with us. Because of this, we can only see what happens where we are. But the eyes of Bosuu the god of the earth are everywhere. If none of us saw who desecrated the cemetery because we were not at the cemetery when it happened, Bosuu whose eyes are everywhere saw which animal, bird of prey or man did what. But now, he would not say this animal, bird of prey or man did this and this animal, bird of prey or man did not do what we suspect it or him of. But Bosuu says Jacob whose pigs we suspect of desecrating the cemetery and Bakam who we also suspect must go and track down the vultures and hyenas that desecrated the cemetery. When they track them down, they should bring them here. By asking them to go and track down the hyenas and vultures that desecrated the cemetery, Bosuu is not saying they are guilty. They are asked to go and find the vultures and hyenas because they are the ones the people suspect to have a hand either directly or indirectly with the desecration of the cemetery. If someone who is not suspected is asked to go and look for the vultures and the hyenas, people would start wondering whether he committed the abomination. When Jacob and Bakam bring the hyenas and the vultures, Bosuu would in the way he chooses show us the faces of the despicable men in our midst that desecrated the cemetery. If then Bosuu says both men are innocent, Bosuu would ask us to compensate them for their travails. If he says only one of them is innocent, the innocent one would be compensated. Now if we know the faces of the despicable men in our midst who committed this sacrilege, we will either kill them or they will flee. If they flee, the long arm of Bosuu would reach them wherever they flee to and he would deal severely with them. Whoever desecrated the earth will never find rest for his feet or buttocks on the earth. So there is no fear that an offender may flee. But if we kill an offender, we may by doing so preempt the punishment Bosuu has for him which presently I do not know.

It is after Bosuu has told us which men desecrated the cemetery that he would tell us their punishment. Now Bosuu has only told me the desecrated bodies must be reburied and they must be reburied with the vultures and hyenas that desecrated the cemetery. That is why they must be tracked down. This is the only way the earth will be appeased.

'You mean the vultures and hyenas that desecrated the cemetery would be buried alive with the desecrated bodies?' someone asked in a voice full of shock.

'Yes,' said the earth priest

'This is strange,' murmured somebody.

'What they did is strange,' murmured another person.

'What of the pigs?' somebody asked.

'We saw the vultures at the cemetery and heard the howling of the hyenas there,' said the earth priest. 'For now, Bosuu is handing down punishment only to those culprits that we know for sure desecrated the cemetery. No one saw the pigs desecrating the cemetery or heard them grunting there. That is why Bosuu has deferred a verdict on them as he deferred on the men who desecrated the cemetery who we don't also know.'

'Do you think Bosuu will say the men that desecrated the cemetery.' should be buried with the desecrated bodies like the vultures and the hyenas?' asked Gochap.

'How dare you speculate on what is in the mind of Bosuu?' the earth priest spat, his one eye rolling round in the most frightening manner. Saying this, he turned his back on the people.

The people hurried away from the shrine, some looking back as if in fear the earth priest was following them.

'Bosuu's assignment to Jacob and Bakam is bizarre,' someone whispered to the person walking near him when they had moved a couple of yards away from the shrine. 'How are they to find the vultures and hyenas? How can vultures and hyenas be buried with human corpses?'

'You should have asked the earth priest all these questions,' said the person he whispered to.

'Ahh...'

'Then shut up.'

'How would Jacob and Bakam find the vultures and hyenas?' another person wondered aloud.

'The vultures and hyenas that desecrated the graves could not have gone far,' someone said.

'Even if they have gone far, Bosuu who has said they must be found and brought to be buried with the desecrated bodies will lead Bakam and Jacob to where they will find them,' somebody said.

'The vultures must still have the red earth of the cemetery in their talons. So the hyenas must still have it in their paws,' said Adubu.

'I don't think it will be so difficult to find the vultures and hyenas that desecrated the cemetery,' said Gochap. 'The carrion-eaters will surely return to the place they found a feast. All Bakam and Jacob need do is to lie in wait for them at the cemetery.'

'Gochap I won't be surprised if I hear you are the cousin of the tortoise,' someone said.

'The order of Bosuu is strange,' said another person.

'All orders by gods are strange and bizarre if you don't know,' said Adubu.

'The gods are always looking for ways to shock us.'

'No, they are always looking for ways to remind us of their divinity.'

'No, they are always looking for ways to mystify us.'

'All the same this order is strange. That since we were born we had seen the sun hanging on nothing in the sky does not stop us marvelling at the strangeness of it all whenever we look at the sun. That we have always seen clouds floating over our heads only to fall as rain later has never failed to mystify us '

'When we understand a god fully we cease to respect him,' someone said after some quiet.

'What Bosuu has decided is strange to our custom,' said another person.

'Custom is a beaten path,' said Gochap. 'We all like to walk on this path because we have no fear of thorns pricking our feet. But the feet that first walked on the path were pricked by thorns. Now we have soft soles. No one wants to walk on a new path and be pricked by thorns.'

'When people invoke custom, it is either they cannot think and decide for themselves or are afraid of thinking and deciding for themselves or stand to benefit from the custom,' said Adubu

'I still say what Bosuu has said has never been heard by our custom,' someone said.

'Bosuu is the custom,' said another person.

'Yoko, you said the decision of Bosuu is strange,' said Gochap, 'since you were born have you ever heard of hyenas, vultures and pigs desecrating graves? We must invent strange customs to meet strange happenings. If a bastard climbs a tree, it is another bastard that is sent to bring him down.'

'The people are the custom and the culture,' said somebody 'and they appear to accept what Bosuu had said. The dead bodies have to be reburied, and the vultures and hyenas with them. For a year, we must bring wine to pour on their graves. Nothing turns the dead from anger like wine.'

'When did Bosuu tell you that one?' someone asked.

'He is an oracle without a shrine and a god. He is part of the strange times we are living in,' said Gochap.

'Since I left the shrine I keep wondering what punishment Bosuu will inflict on the men that desecrated the cemetery,' said Adubu.

'You must be a brave man to still wonder over what the earth priest had said we should not speculate on,' somebody said.

'I believe it was in the shrine the earth priest did not want us to speculate over the punishment Bosuu would mete out on the scoundrels. Now that we have left the shrine, I can wonder and wonder,' said Adubu.

'I agree with you Adubu,' somebody said. 'In my mind, I think Bosuu will say the men, like the vultures and hyenas that desecrated the cemetery, should be buried with the dead bodies they desecrated. That is justice which we all know Bosuu stands for. But if…'

'Shee…' someone hushed the man who was speaking. 'It is sacrilege to speculate on the thinking of Bosuu at length on this matter after what the earth priest said.'

'I agree with you,' said another person. 'We all know that when the earth priest prohibited us from speculating on the mind of Bosuu, he was merely expressing the mind of the god.'

'Those who commit the sacrilege of speculating on the matter would be buried alive with the desecrated bodies,' someone said.

'I am surprised the earth priest did not say the pigs would also be buried with the dead bodies like the vultures and hyenas that desecrated the cemetery,' said another person.

'Maybe it is because the pigs are guiltier that Bosuu has left their case to us knowing our judgment would be harsher,' said Adubu.

'That maybe so, but I suspect Bosuu is loath to deal with the pigs,' said Gochap. 'I have a feeling that pigs will always have their way where the god of the earth is concerned. 'Do you think it is only because of food the pig has its snout to the ground? As a pig noses for food on the ground grunting, it is also pleading with the god of the earth to have mercy. While the vulture is pleading with the god of the sky for mercy for being a carrion-eater, the pig is pleading with the god of the earth for being such a glutton that eats anything including the earth. If you consult the god of the sky over this matter, he is likely to sentence the pigs to death, but would most likely spare the vultures.'

'I don't agree with you Gochap,' somebody said. 'What I can see is that there is a lot of advantage in being filthy. You cannot be used for sacrifice. The pig is too filthy to be used to appease the earth.'

Everyone began to speak what he thought of pigs.

'A pig in shit is a happy pig.'

'Pigs have been given appetite for any kind of food. So they can never suffer hunger for lack of what to eat.'

'With all their weight and awkward limbs, pigs can swim as well, if not better than dogs. So no flood can devour them.'

'From the look of things, very soon, pigs are going to be more skilful in the martial arts than our soldiers.'

'The poison of a snake has no effect on a pig. So a pig can eat a snake tail first. They say snakes strike only people wearing clothes, but flee from naked people because they think they are pigs.'

'The snake that strikes the tortoise on its shell wastes its poison.'

'The itching sap in cocoyam has no effect on the throat of a pig.'

'The pig has no skin you can flay to punish it.'

'A pig in shit is a happy pig.'

'Only the dirty get favours in a dirty world.'

'Everyone looks after his kind.'

'But the vultures and the hyenas are dirty too.'

'Still they are better than the pig. The hyenas and vultures are only dirty within. The pig is dirty within and without.'

'If you look at this matter well, no one is better placed to find the vultures and hyenas than the pigs. For all we know, they desecrated the graves together. So the pigs should be able to point at their fellow felons. It should be easier for them to find their cousins in the forest. Yet, the pigs have been spared the ordeal.'

'But why are we giving the pigs all the bashing? What of the hyenas?' someone swung the talk towards hyenas.

'Hyenas have no relation from whom any gain can be made. No one sows on barren ground.'

'No one invests his hope in a drought. If you invest your hope in a flood you may catch a fish. But whoever invests his hope in a drought can only have the dry wind filing his nostrils. The hyena is a drought.'

'Hyenas are such worthless gluttons. Whenever there is a dispute involving food in the jungle you can be sure the hyena would be there. Why waste time talking about what has no remedy?'

'The hyena looks for food everywhere not because it has a bigger stomach than the leopard, but because it is not able to put a bridle on its stomach like the leopard.'

'I cannot understand the decision of Bosuu that the hyenas and vultures be buried with the dead bodies. If originally the vultures and hyenas were not buried with the corpses, yet they came to eat them, now that they are to be locked up in one room, what would happen?'

'No one will say you have not said something there.'

'As far as I am concerned, the chief's decision is the only relief in the agony we find ourselves. I am looking for stomachs to borrow to eat the moneylender's food.'

'You may soon look for people to lend your stomach to,' said Gochap. 'You don't seem to understand that the judgment of Bosuu has not only exposed the judgment of the chief for what it is, but upturned it. If Jacob and Bakam can go into the forest unmolested by the ghosts of Chuwajo and other dead men, it means anyone can go about fending for himself. Bosuu has exposed the chief for what he is. But that is not your only grief with Bosuu's decision. With Jacob in the forest stalking vultures, there would be no Jacob in the village feeding you.'

What Gochap said shocked everyone. From the reaction of the crowd to what he said, it appeared he was the only one that saw the matter in that light.

'What!' cried someone.

'No, that cannot be,' said another.'

'The earth priest cannot serve us such a cruel joke.'

'For his sake and the sake of his god, he dares not.'

'We have to be alive to get the benefit of the earth being appeased the way Bosuu said it should be appeased.'

'Gochap, you can't be serious!'

'You are saying he is not serious when you should say he is mad. It is only mad men that come up with such eccentric understanding.'

'But what Gochap said is the truth,' someone said.

'It is not always healthy living with the truth,' another person said. 'Sometimes it is healthier living with lies. We will all be mad if we know the truth in certain situations. Lies sometimes are more merciful.'

'Is it only merciful? Sometimes they are more helpful.'

'Is it only sometimes? Always they serve one better.'

'The truth can slay.'

'The truth is a slayer.'

'God created lies and illusions to shield us from the destruction of the truth in certain situations.'

'Why are we joking with a serious matter?' lamented Gochap

'I am not joking,' said the man who first sought to refute what Gochap had said. 'I am only fighting to ensure that my right to eat is respected.'

'The chief is a crook,' someone said.

'If Jacob is a crook, he has found a match in the chief,' said Adubu.

'If the chief is a crook, he has found a match in the earth priest,' said Gochap. The chief now has to go back eating his locusts if he still has them.'

'The earth priest should have consulted the chief before he threw away his food by his decision,' said Adubu.

Chapter Twenty-Four

Jacob left the earth priest's shrine bewildered and with a haunting sense of having come to the end of the road. His life had fallen to ruins on a knoll in a river and the pieces had rolled into the water around the knoll so that he could not pick them even if he wanted to. He had fallen where his pieces could not be picked. In a way, he was now ravaged by problems the way the locusts ravaged his cornfields. Complying with the order of the chief had finished one of his barns and had eaten deep into the second. And now this new sentence by the earth priest.

Like the people had said, the order of the earth priest was bizarre. But it was unthinkable not to comply with it. Well, there was a good side to the sentence of the earth priest. It has released him from the sentence of the chief. He could not be looking for vultures and hyenas in the forest and feeding the village. That he himself would walk the forest without being attacked by a ghost meant anyone could move about and fend for himself. This was where he had come unstuck. This was where his enemies and the chief had fallen flat. The earth priest had sawed off the branch they were sitting and feeding gleefully on him. Still, he could feel the strain of anguish cutting into his brain with the pain of a pin tip on an open wound.

Jacob's brother walked with him looking pensive. What he had always warned Jacob against had finally brought about his ruin. Rearing pigs was like rearing hyenas. Pigs have no hold on their stomachs. Once they are hungry they are capable of committing any mischief to appease their stomachs. But neither the chief nor the earth priest had been fair to Jacob. The punishment of the chief was ridiculous and that of the earth priest bizarre. It looked like both the chief and the earth priest were committed to the destruction of Jacob. None of the punishments handed to his brother was part of the custom of the village he knew. The judgment of the chief was no doubt that of a vulture out to feast on Jacob. Yes, the offence was unknown and sacrilegious, but a heavy fine would have met it. As far as he was concerned, Jacob needed not comply with either the judgment of the chief or that of the earth priest. Let what would happen, happen. As far as he was concerned, Bosuu was a dead god and Jacob needs not submit to the bizarre order of the god. But Jacob was so scared he would not listen to him.

Immediately after leaving the earth priest's shrine, neither brother spoke to the other. While Jacob was full of fear and shock, his brother was reeking with resentment and anger. For a long time Jacob could not think. He just felt numb and dizzy. How are we to find the vultures and hyenas? he kept asking himself when he could think again. If we find the vultures and Bosuu says I also desecrated the cemetery, what punishment would he impose on me? Would he say I should be buried with the desecrated bodies like the vultures and the hyenas? No, no, no. But it is not beyond Bosuu to hand down such a punishment. He might even say I should be buried alive with the desecrated bodies. That maybe the reason he does not want the people to kill the men that desecrated the cemetery. Oh no…'

The crowd of people walking with Jacob and his brother avoided them like plagues when they left the shrine. But as they moved closer to the village, some of the people began to move closer to mock Jacob.

'If people are patient, they will see the end of anything unpleasant,' someone said. 'Similarly, if they are wise, they would know that whenever they are licking what is sweet, their tongues would soon find what is bitter.'

'If people are wise, they will be able to see the end of whatever evil thing they are doing, even if the end is behind a mountain as big as Gugunu,' said another person.

'The very mouth a man eats food can be the mouth that slays his neck. The teeth a man uses to feed his stomach he can also use to dig his grave. The pigs that made Jacob rich yesterday are making him poor today.'

'The mouth has a knife – the tongue, and many diggers – the teeth. The tongue of a fool slays his neck, while the teeth of a glutton dig his grave. Jacob, your teeth have dug your grave.'

'Now that you have to go after vultures and hyenas in the forest who will look after your pigs?'

'This is going to be an interesting expedition. Bakam and Jacob are not friends. How would they prosecute this expedition together?'

'They don't have to do it together. Each I believe would go his own way. Even now do you see them walking together?'

'This is a one-man expedition. Only Bakam can find the vultures.

'Why do you say so?'

'Bakam is a hunter. Besides, I think he is innocent. Only the innocent can be used for sacrifice. I believe Bosuu knows that it is innocence that can track down the vultures and the hyenas and that is why Bakam has been asked to go after them. Bakam is being sacrificed.'

'I don't agree with you that only an innocent man can find the vultures and the hyenas,' someone said rabidly. 'Jacob is a vulture and the vultures would help their own. Have you all forgotten how crocodiles made a bridge for Bundu the evil man to cross the river? The vultures will surely help their own. The vultures do not know Bakam and they will run away from him. In a wicked world, only the wicked prosper. Virtue is fodder to the wicked. For a man of virtue to seek to flourish in a wicked world is like a sheep seeking to prosper in a community of hyenas or a fish seeking to get on well in a crocodile infested river.'

'That is where you are wrong,' said another person. 'The vulture will see Jacob for what he is: A vulture that has escaped from hell that can eat his own kind.'

People walking much nearer Jacob began to make jest of him.

'Jacob, give us money to go and look for the vultures and hyenas for you. You are too soft for this grilling task.'

'Jacob, I tell you this is a world of taking advantage of opportunities.'

'And we are taking ours.'

'Just as you have been taking yours.'

'Just as your namesake in the Bible took his.'

'Jacob, let those who eat with spoons remember those who eat with their fingers.'

'Whoever will go looking for the vultures and the hyenas, let's burn down his house. He does not need it any longer.'

'Jacob, we are going to burn your house when you are gone on Bosuu's errand. You no longer need it. The forest is now your home.'

Jacob's heart plunged.

'If anyone comes near Jacob's house the whole village would burn,' swore Jacob's brother, panting with anger. 'The maize you have been roasting has started exploding. When the kite preys on the bat, it first tears open the bat's wing and clings unto them so that the bat cannot fly. The bat in turn would bite the throat of the kite and not let go. Thus the two would cling to each other in a fight-to-death until each falls to the ground dead and is picked up for meat. We the bats assure the kites that if anyone sets Jacob's house ablaze, our fight will only be resolved in the wooden tray in which our meat would be shared; this time not by men, but by vultures.'

'Certainly, Koyan you seem to be breathing harder than the person suffering from the asthma,' someone said.

'We will call off your bluff and expose it for what it is,' another person said.

'What are you waiting for?'

Chapter Twenty-Five

The bricklayer in the crowd had one fear and one worry. Though he was a Christian, he feared Bosuu the god of the earth. He was under no illusion the god would not catch up with him even if he fled the village. He knew of the line of fire in the shrine. He also knew what happened to Boma who stole yam and Zokom who defiled the river. His sacrilege was more than those committed by Zokom and Boma and so the god would strike him more severely. His worry was that he had implicated Bakam in a sacrilege he knew nothing about and Bakam was now suffering because of that. He was worse than Judas. The man who had found his money and returned it to him was now in distress because of his treachery. In the earth priest's shrine, he wanted to proclaim to the hearing of everyone that Bakam was innocent and he was the despicable person that desecrated Chuwajo's grave, but his courage had failed him. His only consolation was that he knew most people thought Bakam was innocent. But it would have been wonderful for the people to hear his innocence being declared by the villain who had implicated him in the heinous act. But it was good that he did not succeed in letting Jacob off the hook. Jacob who had so cheated him. Looking at the matter now, he was foolhardy to have thought he could free Jacob from the sacrilege committed by his pigs by simply effacing traces of their visit to the cemetery. Even if he had succeeded in doing so, Bosuu who saw the pigs desecrating Chuwajo's grave would still have fingered them among the culprits that desecrated the cemetery. The earth priest had talked of men who desecrated the cemetery and not the man who desecrated the cemetery. This meant beside him there were other men or at least another man who desecrated the cemetery. Who could that be? Could it be Jacob? Most likely. If he could do what he did for the moneylender, the moneylender would do more for himself. Well, whoever it was must be a contemptible person like him for lacking the courage to own up to his guilt in public. Well, at least he was not the only coward. But what did this other man do? Besides what he, Nathaniel did, there was only evidence of the hyenas' desecration, but no evidence of what the other man did. Did he bring in the hyenas? Well, the important thing was that he did not stand alone in his infamy. Someone was standing with him. But his case was worse. He had implicated an innocent man. The other culprit only implicated hyenas. But he had implicated not only an innocent man, but an innocent man that found his money and returned it to him. Suddenly he felt his head climbing higher and higher into the sky. When his head returned from the sky, he was running through the crowd proclaiming, 'Bakam is innocent. I mutilated Chuwajo's corpse and loaded his hand with ash. What you saw in the grave was ash not gunpowder!'

People quickly stepped out of his way.

'The mad man is at it again,' someone said.

'This is not the madness you know with the bricklayer,' said another man. 'There is something in this madness.'

Could Bosuu the god of the earth have moved so swiftly to hand down justice? most of the people wondered.

The bricklayer ran through the people repeating that he desecrated Chuwajo's grave and he did so to help Jacob who he had now found out was a crook.

Two people tried to hold him, but he shoved them violently aside and ran on, proclaiming his chilling confession.

The people moved on towards the village in a more sober mood. In the village, each man when he got to the path leading to his house branched off the main road, sometime alone, sometime with a friend.

Jacob and his brother branched off towards Jacob's house. 'To be buried alive with vultures and hyenas,' Jacob murmured in deep thought.

'What did you say?' asked the brother.

'No, no, no.'

'What is it?'

'I will kill myself, before the earth priest lays his hands on me?'

'Jacob I don't understand you,' said the brother in a grave tone. 'You are supposed to be a Christian; why should you take the earth priest seriously? Besides, it was your pigs that desecrated the cemetery, so why should you be buried alive with vultures and hyenas?'

'You will not understand,' murmured Jacob. 'It is not as simple as you think.'

'Unless there is something you have not told me, I think I understand,' said the brother.

'What do you mean by that?' asked Jacob, turning sharply to look at his brother.

'I mean unless you went to the cemetery to bury what your pigs did and in the process desecrated the cemetery, you have nothing to fear from the earth priest who you seem to dread so much.'

'I did not go to the cemetery.'

'Then you have nothing to fear.'

'My money, my food all gone,' wept Jacob.'

'I told you not to comply with the ridiculous order, but you would not listen to me,' said the brother. 'The problem with you is that you think you are the only person who knows what is right. I told you, no bastard dares come near you or any of your possessions because you have not obeyed the chief's order, but fear would not allow you to defy the chief and his ridiculous judgment. See the result.'

'My money… my pigs… my maize. I have nothing left.'

'You have me, your wife and your son,' said the brother soothingly.

'Wife? Without my money, she would be gone before you blink your eyes. My millet…'

'Jacob, you are behaving as timidly as the vulture you said you are. Behave like a hawk and I tell you no rat will come near you to do you harm.'

'It is so fearful and stressful.'

'I believe what you need is something to eat and a good sleep,' said the brother.

'What is the matter with you? Didn't you hear the sentence of Bosuu the god of the earth?'

'Like I told you earlier, I am a Christian and Bosuu is nothing better than the ground I walk on. If I fear to tread on the earth, I will fear Bosuu.'

'Shee…'Jacob muttered, shrinking his body in fear. 'You are a small boy. These things are more potent than you think. We have to make haste and go to the forest. 'Who knows, we might be lucky to track these vultures down today. They are not likely to have wandered far.'

'You can be sure I will not be a party to your compliance with that bizarre order,' the brother said, 'All I want for you now is something to eat and a good rest. You have not eaten anything today. Let's enter the house and see if there is something to eat.' He began pulling his brother towards the house.

'My money… my millet,' cried Jacob.

'Let's go,' repeated the brother tugging Jacob who appeared unwilling to enter the house.

'Let's go where?' asked Jacob.

Jacob's brother wondering why his brother was asking him such a question stepped back and looked at Jacob. What he saw was not the Jacob he knew. Jacob's eyes were pasty and he looked faint. Holding him by the hand, he said, 'let's go in and see if there is something to eat.'

'Something to eat ...'

Shaking his head, the brother left him outside and went inside the house. Soon he was out with his hands on his head crying, 'the pigs! They have all been killed. Oh Jacob!'

Jacob staggered forward. His brother to stop him from falling rushed and caught him by his hand, but Jacob twisted and fell on his back. His brother raised him up to a sitting position and propped him up against his body. Jacob was sweating and his breathing was fast and shallow. His face was drawn and his eyes were limp. With both men sitting on the ground, Jacob's brother was trying to console him by talking to him, but it was not clear if Jacob whose eyes were on the ground in front of him heard him.

After a long while of fixing his eyes on the ground, Jacob looked up and saw two vultures flying towards him.

'Koyan, look at the vultures I want to go in search of,' he cried, pointing at the sky.

Jacob's brother looked at the direction his brother was pointing and to his shock saw two vultures flying low in a band that reminded him of the locusts attack. Beyond the vultures, he could see the bricklayer wielding a machete and dancing towards them shouting.

'Jacob here are the vultures that desecrated the cemetery with your pigs!'

THE END

Printed in the United States
By Bookmasters